"Vivian, you're just asking for trouble."

"That means I don't scare you," she said in a sultry voice.

"You scare the hell out of me because I shouldn't like dancing with you. I shouldn't like flirting with you. I shouldn't want to kiss you. I shouldn't feel anything when our fingers touch, and neither should you."

"For a US Army Ranger, you're a little stuffy."

He caught her around the waist and took long steps, dancing in circles through the terrace doors and outside, where it was darker and cooler.

"Try this for stuffy, darlin'." He pulled her tightly against him and his mouth covered hers as he kissed her. He knew he shouldn't, but he was having more fun with her than he could recall having had anywhere, anytime in the past three years.

* * *

Expecting a Lone Star Heir is part of the Texas Promises trilogy: When three military men return to Texas to fulfill their promises to a fallen comrade, they find redemption...and love.

Dear Reader,

An honorable man keeps his promises, and this series is about three friends keeping promises made to their dying US Army Ranger buddy. The surviving rangers eventually go home to do the honorable thing, and each promise they fulfill involves a life-changing event.

The first to keep his promise is former US Army Ranger Mike Moretti. Mike takes over running his deceased friend's ranch, a situation he doesn't like, but he gave his word. The widow, Vivian Warner, a stunning blonde, knows nothing about ranching— Mike has to work for her, run her spread and try to fight the instant mutual attraction that flares when they meet.

Mike is a cowboy, a rugged alpha male who has definite ideas about relationships, and he sees no place in his life for Vivian. Her father is a billionaire and she has just inherited her deceased husband's multimillionaire fortune. To Mike, Vivian is off-limits.

Vivian fights the attraction because she loved her husband and isn't over the loss. In addition, she knows how Mike feels about her fortune. Mike never imagined he would fall in love with an heiress. Vivian thought her heart was torn away when she lost her husband. This is a story of two people divided by their deep feelings and life views as they fight falling in love.

Thank you for your interest in this book and best wishes to you. Please find me at saraorwig.com or on Facebook as Sara Orwig, Romance Writer.

Sara Orwig

SARA ORWIG

EXPECTING A LONE STAR HEIR

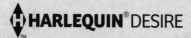

H**HARLEQUIN**® DESIRE

Recycling programs
for this product may
not exist in your area.

ISBN-13: 978-0-373-83881-3

Expecting a Lone Star Heir

Copyright © 2017 by Sara Orwig

This edition published by arrangement with Harlequin Books S.A.

For questions and comments about the quality of this book, please contact us at CustomerService@Harlequin.com.

® and TM are trademarks of Harlequin Enterprises Limited or its corporate affiliates. Trademarks indicated with ® are registered in the United States Patent and Trademark Office, the Canadian Intellectual Property Office and in other countries.

Printed in U.S.A.

www.Harlequin.com

Sara Orwig, from Oklahoma, loves family, friends, dogs, books, long walks, sunny beaches and palm trees. She is married to and in love with the guy she met in college. They have three children and six grandchildren. Sara's 100th published novel was a July 2016 release. With a master's degree in English, Sara has written historical romance, mainstream fiction and contemporary romance. Sara welcomes readers on Facebook or at saraorwig.com.

Books by Sara Orwig

Harlequin Desire

Lone Star Legends

The Texan's Forbidden Fiancée
A Texan in Her Bed
At the Rancher's Request
Kissed by a Rancher
The Rancher's Secret Son
That Night with the Rich Rancher

Callahan's Clan

Expecting the Rancher's Child
The Rancher's Baby Bargain
The Rancher's Cinderella Bride
The Texan's Baby Proposal

Texas Promises

Expecting a Lone Star Heir

Visit her Author Profile page at Harlequin.com, or saraorwig.com, for more titles.

To senior editor Stacy Boyd
with many, many thanks.

To Maureen Walters,
as always, with thanks.

To my family,
who are all-important to me.

To my friends,
who have given me laughter and memories.

To hope, to love and to peace.

Prologue

Afghanistan, November

What else could go wrong?

In the dark, under a starless sky, they had driven their Humvee straight into an ambush, and now they were barely holding on, pinned down in a firefight with nothing but a crumbling rock wall between them and the enemy. Help couldn't arrive too soon.

Mike Moretti was one of the lucky ones—he only had cuts and bruises. His two close friends, Noah Grant and Jake Ralston, also had non-life-threatening injuries. The other member on this US Army Rangers mission, Captain Thane Warner, wasn't so lucky. Mike didn't need a doctor to tell him that Thane was hurt badly with wounds to his chest and head, an injured leg and deep gashes all over his body from flying shrapnel. Mike was trying to apply pressure to the two most serious wounds, hoping his captain and friend would hang on until help arrived. Their last communication had been cut off, but before it was he'd been told a chopper was on the way.

Thane gripped his arm and Mike leaned closer to hear him over the gunfire. His voice was raspy, his breathing shallow as he spoke through the pain that was no doubt seizing his body. "Mike, promise me you'll take the ranch job for three months at least. Promise me you'll work for Vivian. I want to know she's taken care of when I'm gone." Coughs racked his body and he grimaced. "Promise me."

"I promise," Mike said without thinking. He concentrated on trying to keep pressure on the wounds.

Thane grabbed his arm with a strength that shocked Mike as Thane pulled him closer. "Key... in my pocket... Get it."

Mike heard the desperation in the captain's voice, felt it in his grip. But he couldn't ease up the pressure on these deep wounds or the man would surely bleed out before a medic got to him. When Thane began to struggle, trying to get to his pocket himself, the bleeding worsened, oozing over Mike's hand.

"Be still. I'll get the damn key," Mike ordered.

He struggled to get the key out of Thane's back pocket—he bent closer to Thane and reassured him. "I have the key."

Thane squeezed his eyes shut and let out a shaky breath. When he reopened them, Mike saw the gratitude and the fear as clearly as if the captain had spoken the words. "Bottom of box... Packets addressed to Vivian and to you." He grimaced as the pain no doubt intensified, but he wouldn't be deterred. "Get Noah... Need him."

Mike shook his head. "If I leave you, you'll bleed to death."

As an explosion rocked the ground not twenty feet away, sending up a plume of light, Thane placed one hand over the mound of Mike's jacket pressed against his bleeding chest wound. "Get him, dammit."

Swearing, Mike turned to the man next to him and punched his shoulder to draw his attention. There was no use calling out; his voice wouldn't be heard over the gunfire.

As Noah Grant lowered his weapon, Mike told him, "Trade places. Keep pressure on his wounds. He wants to talk to you."

Without hesitation, Noah sidled up to the captain and Mike took up his weapon to keep up the barrage on the enemy, all the time hoping against hope they'd be able to get the injured man on that chopper. His eyes scanned the dark sky. Where was it?

Thane Warner wasn't only his captain; he was a good friend. Back home, Mike had dated Thane's younger sister. Though he'd gotten along with the divorcee's young child, their relationship hadn't lasted. But Mike's friendship with Thane had.

He glanced over his shoulder and saw Noah motioning him over.

"He's drifting in and out of consciousness now," Noah said, shaking his head. "But he wants Jake."

Before Mike could move to get their friend, he heard it—the unmistakable sound of a helicopter in the distance. He pointed his index finger up. "Listen. Chopper." But he still didn't have eyes on it, and Mike couldn't help but wonder if it would be able to get their captain out in time.

If not, Mike admitted with a sinking realization, he had made a promise to Captain Thane Warner and he intended to keep it.

One

After driving past miles of mesquite, dry creek beds and cacti, Mike turned and stopped at a pair of tall wrought iron gates. As soon as he punched in the code he had been given, the gates slid open and he drove through beneath a high ornate iron arch that claimed this to be the Tumbling T Ranch.

Eight miles from the state road, he saw fenced grounds ahead. Among the trees, ponds and white fences was what looked like a small town of houses, offices, barns and outbuildings, all dominated by a stately mansion. The grand home reminded Mike again of Thane Warner's millionaire status and his wife's family of billionaires. As if Mike needed the reminder.

He soon wound up the long drive to the front of the sprawling three-story stone home with slate roofs and wings built on the east and west sides.

He swore quietly. He didn't want this job. It was one thing to accept Thane's offer to go to work on the Warner spread when they expected to come home and work together. It was another to return to civilian life and run a ranch for a widow he didn't know and who didn't know ranching.

It had been last year when Thane had first asked Mike to think about a job on the Tumbling T Ranch. Thane's older foreman had had back trouble and had decided to retire. The foreman had said he would wait until Thane was out of the military and had time to hire someone to take his place. Mike had planned to get a job working on a ranch once he was discharged, so why not work for a man he'd come to like and admire? Besides, the job came with a good salary.

But Thane didn't make it back home.

Mike cast his eyes on the sprawling ranch, as he recalled the days following his friend's death. He had followed Thane's request and used the key Thane had given him to open a lockbox he'd stored in their makeshift camp. Opening the box, he found an odd assortment of stuff, including Thane's cotton T-shirts, some socks, and in the bottom, three fat packets wrapped in wrinkled, torn brown paper and tied with twine. One was addressed to Mike, one to

Noah and one to Jake. Mike passed them out. When he opened his envelope he read a note scribbled on a piece of torn brown paper: *Mike, please give this to Vivian.* He looked at his friends as he held up another envelope. "I'm to take this home to his wife."

Noah scratched his jaw that was covered in black stubble. "Yeah, I'm to take one to his sister."

Noah and Mike looked at Jake who held up his brown envelope. "And I'm to take this to someone who works for his dad." They all looked at each other and Mike guessed his friends were feeling the same as he was.

"Thane was the best," he said. "We've got to do what he wanted."

The others nodded and moved away to stash the envelopes safely until they could get home. Mike knew he was the only one who had another note in the box. That note informed him there was a packet for him hidden in among Thane's things. Mike rummaged through the lockbox and found it quickly. A thick packet shoved down in the toes of a well-worn army sock. Mike opened the fat brown envelope and found more brown paper tied in twine. This one had a note in Thane's handwriting: *Mike, you are the only one getting this. It is yours now. I won't ever miss it. You'll earn it. Please take the other packet to Vivian.*

Mike unwrapped the brown paper to find a stack of bills. He stared at them a moment in shock. He picked up one and looked at it closely. It was a one-thousand dollar bill. He'd never even seen one before. He thumbed through the stack of twenty-five.

He read Thane's note again and shook his head. He didn't know why Thane had given him the gift. It was no secret that Thane came from a wealthy family. Along with his two brothers and sister, he was a multimillionaire, and his wife a billionaire heiress, so Thane would never have needed the money if he had lived, but it still was an odd gift. Mike shook his head again, wondering if Thane thought he was poverty-stricken since he was the only one of their group of four friends who wasn't a millionaire. No, he knew that wasn't the case because Thane was practical and Mike had never known him to throw money away. That day, and every day since, each time he looked at the bills, he thought of Thane and wanted his friend with him instead of the money.

Now with Thane gone, the foreman job didn't appeal to Mike, but a promise was a promise. Mike wasn't going back on his word.

From scuttlebutt and by piecing together things Thane had said, Mike knew Thane's artist wife was the daughter of a billionaire Dallas hotel magnate, plus now she had inherited Thane's millions from his ranch and oil interests. Vivian and Thane had only been married a few months when he'd left for Afghanistan. She knew nothing about ranching and Thane had constantly worried about her. Also, he hated to think that if something happened to him, she would sell the ranch and return home to Dallas where she had lived when she was single.

As he stepped out of the car, he pulled on his western-cut navy jacket. His gaze ran over the sprawling gray stone mansion that looked as if it should be in an exclusive Dallas suburb instead of sitting on a mesquite-covered prairie. The mansion was surrounded by beds of spring flowers. Beyond the beds was lush green grass that had to be watered constantly in the dry Texas heat. A tall black wrought iron fence with open gates circled the mansion yard.

After running his fingers through his wavy ebony hair, Mike put on his broad-brimmed black Stetson. As he strode to the front door, he realized he had felt less reluctance walking through minefields in Afghanistan. He crossed the wide porch that held steel and glass furniture with colorful cushions, pots of greenery and fresh flowers. He listened to the door chimes and in seconds, the ten-foot intricately carved wooden door swung open. He faced an actual butler.

"I'm Mike Moretti. I have an appointment with Mrs. Warner."

"Ah, yes, we're expecting you. Come in. I'm Henry, sir."

Mike stepped into a wide entryway with a huge crystal chandelier centered overhead above a small pond where a fountain splashed and deep purple and bright pink water lilies added to the ambiance. It was hard to picture the down-to-earth, tough US Army Ranger, Thane Warner as the owner of this elegant mansion.

"If you'll wait here, sir, I'll tell Mrs. Warner you've arrived."

"Thank you," Mike replied, nodding at the butler

who turned and disappeared into a room off the hall. With neatly trimmed brown hair, Henry wore a white shirt and a matching black tie and trousers. Mike noticed he also wore boots and when he had shown Mike in, his hands looked rough. His shoulders were thick and broad. Mike suspected Henry might not spend all his time working inside the mansion.

He reappeared. "If you'll come with me, sir, Mrs. Warner is in the study." Mike followed him until Henry stopped at an open door. "Mrs. Warner, this is Mike Moretti."

"Come in, Mr. Moretti," she said, smiling as she walked toward him.

He entered a room filled with floor-to-ceiling shelves of leather-bound books. After the first glance, he forgot his surroundings and focused solely on the woman approaching him.

Mike had seen Thane's pictures of his wife—one in his billfold, one he carried in his duffel bag. Mike knew from those pictures that she was pretty. But those pictures hadn't done her justice, because in real life, Vivian Warner was a downright beauty. She had big blue eyes, shoulder-length blond hair, flawless peaches-and-cream complexion and full rosy lips. The bulky, conservative tan sweater and slacks she wore couldn't fully hide her womanly curves and long legs.

What had he gotten himself into? For a moment he was tempted to go back on his promise. But as always, he would remember those last hours with Thane's blood running over his hands, recall too easily Thane dying in a foreign land after fighting for his country, and Mike knew he had to keep his promise. His only hope was that Thane's widow wouldn't want him to work for her.

"Mr. Moretti, I'm glad to meet you. I've heard so much about you from Thane," she said, offering her hand.

"It's Mike," he said, smiling as he took her soft hand in his. The moment he did, he felt a tingling up his arm that shocked him.

"And I'm Vivian," she said, her eyes widening when his hand wrapped around hers. Her words came out breathlessly, making Mike feel he had walked into a major disaster. Their gazes locked and he couldn't get his breath, either. For a moment he felt a hot, intense awareness of her as a woman. A very desirable woman. And judging by her startled expression and the quick intake of her breath, he had a feeling she felt a similar reaction.

His focus shifted to her lips, a rosy temptation. Realizing they were staring at each other and standing too close, he released her hand. When he did, she stepped back, looking suddenly uncomfortable. Perhaps she labeled the attraction as unwanted as he did.

"I'm sorry for your loss," Mike said. "Your husband was a friend I'll miss," he added, trying to get his mind back to Thane instead of on his widow.

"Thank you. Thane was special. Please have a seat," she said softly. She walked toward an arrangement of chairs and as he followed, he couldn't take his eyes off the curve of her hips.

Mike did not want this scalding awareness of his late buddy's wife. And he damn well didn't want to work for Vivian Warner.

Perhaps... He couldn't help the thought that overtook his mind. Perhaps, because she knew so little about ranching, if he took the job, she would turn running the ranch over to him and he would seldom see or talk to her. Maybe, but... Common sense told him to thank her for the job and decline the offer. But each time he thought about backing off, he knew he had to keep his promise. Thane had fought and died not only for rights, freedom and home, but for promises kept and for trusted friends. He had fought for this ranch he loved and the wife he loved. Mike also thought about that fat packet of money Thane had given him, money he'd already squirreled away and invested.

Mike would do what he felt was right, but he hoped with all his being that he rarely ever saw his new boss. This was not the woman for him and there were more than a billion reasons—each and every one of the billions she was worth. Vivian Warner was an heiress, his friend's wife, the woman Thane had entrusted to him to take care of. He couldn't give in to the fiery attraction and seduce her—and betray that trust. For all those reasons, she was off-limits, not the least of which was the fact that he could never move in her circle.

Vivian motioned him to a brown leather wingback chair, then sat farther away than was necessary. He realized that she may have felt as trapped by this situation as he did. Thane had offered him the job and had wanted him as the foreman. Like Mike, she obviously was also following Thane's wishes now.

"Thank you for taking this job," she said, her voice lilting, soft-spoken. "Thane wrote a glowing letter about you and said I could count on you to run this place the way he would want. I appreciate that. I know you accepted the job when you were still in the military. Now that you're here, I assume that means you want the job. Is that correct?"

Her question hung in the air but he couldn't say yes. "I promised Thane I would take the job for three months to see if I fit and vice versa," he reluctantly answered.

"So you're here on a trial basis," she said, her smile vanishing, and he merely nodded. "Thane had great trust in you so I hope you like it here and stay," she continued. "Slade Jackson, our foreman, wants to retire and I can't run this ranch. Actually, Slade runs this place as if it's his ranch and that's what Thane said you would do."

"That makes my job easier," Mike answered, wondering how often he would see her once he started work. He would have to report in, let her know what was going on, but that didn't have to be a daily occurrence or even by direct contact. Email would be a salvation.

"There's a house on the ranch for the foreman. In fact, most of the men who work here live on the ranch." She crossed her legs and sat back in her chair. "I don't know what Thane told you about me. I'm

an artist and I own a gallery in Dallas where I show
and sell my paintings. They're also shown in three
other galleries in Houston, Austin and Santa Fe, New
Mexico. That takes a lot of my time and I know little
about the ranch. We have an accountant and his assistant who help with the bills and payroll. There are
two cowboys working here who also double, when
needed, as chauffeurs. You'll see the limo in the garage. There's a landing strip and we have two planes
and again, three of the cowboys are pilots. I saw on
your résumé that you have a pilot's license."

"That's correct."

She nodded her approval. "We have a chef and
also the wife of one of the men is a cook for the employees who live here. My cook, Francie Ellison, is
here five days a week, off on the weekends unless
there's something special. She has an apartment on
the third floor. Heather, the woman who is in charge
of the cleaning crew also has an apartment on that
floor, and Waldo, her husband, is in charge of the
gardening crew. I don't live alone in this house, Mr.
Moretti."

"Just call me Mike."

Vivian Warner sat a little straighter and locked
her fingers together. "I have a couple of problems.
I think one will vanish the minute I introduce you.
Since I'm isolated on the ranch and everyone in the
area knows I'm a widow and alone, the issues are
with two men in particular. I don't think it will ever
involve you and I'm not afraid of either one because
I don't feel threatened, just annoyed. Also, when

Thane knew he would be away and I would be isolated, my father talked to him about a bodyguard and Thane agreed I should have one—even when other people live in the house. With my family background, I might be a tempting target. So I have a bodyguard—he and his wife live in this house, too. That way, he's close at hand."

"Henry is the bodyguard, isn't he?"

"Yes," she said, tilting her head as she gazed at him. "Thane told you there was a bodyguard?"

"No. Henry didn't look like my idea of a man who spends every working hour as a butler."

"You're observant. Henry Paine and his wife, Millie, live in this house on the third floor. I feel Henry can do a better job as my bodyguard if he's in the house."

"I agree with that."

She smiled. "His wife, Millie, is my assistant and helps with the business part of my art. As far as the problems I have, Thane knew nothing about them because he had enough to worry about where he was. I didn't want him halfway around the world and worrying about me and two men I can cope with well enough. With you taking this job, I think the least of the two problems will vanish instantly because it didn't exist when Thane was here. It concerns one of my employees." She ran a hand over her blond hair, more of a nervous gesture, Mike thought, since not one strand was out of place. Then she continued. "Thane always said Leon Major could work with horses better than any other cowboy he had known.

Thane let Leon deal with the problem horses that he wanted to keep, so I don't want to let Leon go. I also haven't ever told this to Slade. Slade isn't well, plus he's older, so I didn't want to worry him. Besides, Leon isn't threatening. He's more of a nuisance. Since Thane's death, he's been by to see me a couple of times. At first, I thought it was about the ranch or business."

"And it wasn't at all," Mike said, and she nodded.

"I told him not to come to the house. He can talk to Slade, our foreman. So far, Leon has cooperated and as I said, with your taking the job, I think that will be the end of that problem."

"What's the other problem?"

"That's a bigger one, unfortunately. My neighbor, Clint Woodson, knows I'm widowed and knows I'm not a rancher. He's divorced and he wants me to go out with him. I also know he wants this ranch."

"Are you interested in selling?"

"At this point, no, I'm not. The time may come when I will be, but I don't want to do something in haste and regret it later. Also, if I don't sell to him and I won't go out with him, I keep thinking he'll stop coming by or calling me. Neither man, not Leon nor my neighbor, has stepped out of line to the extent that Henry would get involved with, so I haven't had any help from Henry about this except to make his presence known. You see, Mr. Moretti, I haven't gone out with any man since Thane, nor have I wanted to. There are other men who've called, but some are simply friends who are being nice and asking me out since I'm widowed and don't get out much. Some are a nuisance, but I can deal with that. Actually, Clint started asking me out as soon as Thane enlisted. Since Thane's death, Clint calls and drops by much more often. I don't invite him inside and Henry always makes an appearance. Occasionally, he comes by when Henry has gone to town—it's as if he knows when Henry leaves—but I don't even go to the door. I'm not afraid of Clint. He's just aggravating and I don't care to talk to him. He brings me presents, which I tell him I can't accept, so he leaves them on the porch. I give them to a charity in town and tell them to drop him a thank-you, but that hasn't stopped him. Nor have I managed to convince him that I have no interest in going out with him or selling this ranch to him."

Mike nodded. "When I'm in charge, we can keep him from setting foot on the ranch. We can stop him at the front gate and tell him you're not receiving visitors. I can also go into town and get to know the sheriff so there won't be any misunderstandings. You can think about that last one."

"I don't need to think about it. That would be excellent if it works. I've thought about changing the code but with the amount of people who live and work here, he can easily get it from one of them. And we usually have the gate open anyway."

"We can hire someone to be a gatekeeper temporarily. Or perhaps we could get several hands who are willing to do extra duty."

She nodded. "We'll see if that works." Then she

added some further information about the neighboring suitor. "As soon as Thane had to deploy, Clint started being buddies with my dad. They have mutual friends, you see. My dad's business is hotels, but he does have an oil company, so he and Clint know each other in the business world, too. It won't matter. I just wanted you to know. I can take care of my dad."

"It shouldn't take long to get the message across," Mike reassured her.

Her shoulders seemed to ease and a small smile pulled back her lips. "Thane wrote a very long, detailed glowing letter about how much he trusted you and how much I can trust you."

Mike looked into her eyes and wondered how many times he would have to remind himself how much Thane had trusted him. "Thane was a buddy, a fine man, and I trusted him with my life. I'm sorry he didn't make it home."

She looked away and laced her fingers together in her lap. "I am, too. I miss him." As she stared into space he waited silently. Finally, she turned to look at him again.

"How soon can you start work? I'll tell you that we need you today, or as soon as you can start working here."

"I can start tomorrow. Because of being in the military, I travel lightly, so I can move in right away."

"That's wonderful. You can have the guesthouse as long as Slade is still here. When he goes, we'll have the foreman house done over however you'd like and you can move in there."

"Sounds good to me," he said. There was a moment of silence and she looked as if she were debating whether or not to say something so he sat quietly waiting.

"I want to ask you something. If you don't want to do this, say no."

"Sure. Ask away," he said, curious of what she had in mind.

"After you've worked here a couple of weeks, could we go out to dinner maybe a few times where people would see us?" She took a deep breath. "You don't have to agree, but I think if you went out with me where we would be seen, Clint and a couple of the other men who have called on me would back off. I think Clint would stop trying to get me to move and sell the ranch. We could go to a country club in Dallas—dinner will go on my tab, of course, because, in the first place, at the club that's automatic." Her cheeks turned pink as she talked. "You don't have to go. It is definitely not a job requirement, and if there's a woman in your life—"

"Relax, Mrs. Warner. I can easily take you to dinner," he lied, trying to sound positive and knowing that she was right about the men backing off. "There's no woman to worry about. You pick the time for dinner and you select the place because you know this neck of the woods better than I do," he said.

They would go to dinner. If it had been anyone besides Thane's wife, he probably would have politely refused, but he believed the reasons she was giving.

When she looked down at her fingers locked together, his gaze swept over her and his heartbeat sped up. Her long blond hair curled slightly where it fell on her shoulders. Mike knew she had no romantic interest in him, but with the jolt of mutual awareness when their hands had briefly touched, he suspected that any time spent with her he would be driven by two forces: the first—intense attraction; the second—the reminder that she was absolutely off-limits for him. She was Thane's wife. How many times had he already had to remind himself of that? It was easy to get lost in those big eyes and forget the world and his purpose here.

"If it looks as if we're dating, I think Clint will stop trying to buy this place. But it's merely a request and if you say no, I'll understand," she repeated.

"As I said, I don't mind taking you to dinner," he lied again politely as he smiled at her.

She looked as if a weight had lifted off her shoulders while he felt as if one had just dropped on his.

"It will help, too, if you'll call me Vivian."

"I noticed Henry calls you Mrs. Warner."

"He did that for your benefit and because you're new. He and his wife both call me Vivian, and Thane told them to call him by his first name. Thane wasn't much for formalities."

"I think it should be Mrs. Warner until we have that dinner date. I'll change to Vivian then."

She nodded. "Thank you for agreeing to dinner.

And remember, it will be the weekend after this one. I have tickets for a charity ball. It's a dinner dance at a country club in Dallas. You'll need a tux."

"I can get one," he said, smiling.

"Good. Clint belongs to the same club, so there's a good chance he'll be there." She shrugged her delicate shoulders. "It's uncanny, but he seems to know most places I go and he appears there, too."

"You haven't noticed anyone following you around when you're off the ranch, have you? He could easily hire a PI."

"No, but I haven't really paid much attention." She smiled at him. "Actually, I'm not off the ranch much because I'm busy painting. I have a showing coming up this month."

"Well, I don't want you to worry about Clint. I think I can get rid of him."

"Thank you, Mike. That's a relief. He's even had real estate people call me about the ranch, as well as an attorney who represents him. It will be such a relief to have him out of my life."

"I don't think that will be difficult to accomplish," Mike replied, already suspecting his biggest problem might be keeping his distance from her.

"I can introduce you to Slade now if you'd like. He's expecting us. He'll talk to you a little and show you around."

"Thane said he has back trouble. Can he still work and get around?"

"Yes, thank goodness. He isn't able to do what he used to, but he works. He does more than he should.

Thane wrote to him and told him how you know ranching. He's glad you're here. We all are." She started to rise from her chair. "I'll call him and we'll go to his office."

"Mrs. Warner, wait a minute," Mike said, wondering how the next few minutes would go. "In the last moments I was with your husband, he asked me to give something to you. He had a gift for you. He kept it with his things. Fighting like we were and on the move, we carried very little with us, but he carried your gift with him. It wasn't gift wrapped. When I brought it home, I thought about having it wrapped. Perhaps it should be, but I thought about all we went through and decided maybe it would mean something special to you to give it to you the way he carried it through fights and tough assignments. I've brought it to you like I got it from him," Mike said, standing. "It seemed more appropriate to me."

"We weren't even married a year," she said, looking at Mike's hands as he pulled the parcel from his jacket pocket. The package was wrapped in plain wrinkled brown paper that was smudged, slightly torn in a couple of spots. He held it out to her. She glanced up at him and then took it from him with icy fingers.

"Thane had this?"

"Yes, for you. I imagine he got it when we were in one of the European cities. I don't know when or where. We never talked about it, really, except when he asked me to get it to you."

She struggled with the string until he reached into

his pocket. "Here, let me," he said, opening a small knife and cutting the twine. Their fingers brushed and again, Mike had that instant sizzle when there should have been nothing. Without thinking, he glanced from the package to her and saw her surprised look again as she gazed up at him. The minute he met her eyes, she hurried to unwrap the wrinkled brown paper.

When she saw the gift, she gasped. A gold chain with a large diamond pendant glittered in the light. It looked like an antique. She closed her hand around the necklace and put her head down. To give her privacy, he walked a few feet away to a window to gaze outside without seeing anything before him. Instead, he remembered the flashes of shells and flames, the smell of blood and fire and gunpowder. He remembered Thane and hurt again over the loss of his friend.

"There's a note," she said. He didn't turn to look. He could hear her open paper and then she was quiet. And he knew she was crying because she loved her husband. "Sorry," she whispered.

"Don't be. We all miss him, including Noah and Jake, our two other friends. Thane bought that pendant for you because he loved you. He was a good man and people cry over good men."

Mike moved away, returning to his seat and looking at his phone, trying to give her a moment until she was ready to talk again.

"I always thought he would come home to me. I

was sure he'd get through it," she said so softly, he could barely hear her. "I was wrong."

Mike stood. "I'll get you a drink of water," he said, leaving so she could be alone with her grief for a few minutes. He hadn't been in the hall two seconds before Henry emerged from one of the rooms.

"Can I help you, Mr. Moretti?"

"It's Mike, Henry. She told me you're a bodyguard. You're military, too, aren't you?"

"Yes, sir. Marines."

"I'm giving her a moment. I told her I'd get her a drink of water. Thane had a gift for her and a note, and asked me to give it to her. It… Well, it tore her up."

"I'll get the water. Have a seat, Mike."

Mike smiled and felt he would have a friend in Henry.

In minutes Henry returned with a tray that held two glasses and a pitcher of ice water. Cubes clinked in the pitcher as he approached Mike. "Here's one for you, sir."

"Henry, you don't need to call me 'sir.'"

"Yes, sir. Not too many people off the ranch realize I'm anything but a butler out here. It's probably better that way. As you know, she's worth a lot and this can be an isolated spot in spite of all the people who work here."

"Okay. I'll take the water to her. She should be okay now."

Henry held the door open and closed it quietly

behind Mike. Vivian was at the window and turned to face him.

He crossed the room and held the tray for her. "Have a drink."

"Thanks. That caught me off guard," she said, taking the glass nearest her. "I loved him and I miss him."

"That's understandable." Mike turned away to set the tray on a table and sip his drink. He set the glass back on the tray.

"If you're ready now, I'll call Slade and see if he's ready to meet you."

"Sure, go ahead."

While she talked on her phone, he glanced around. The desk at one side of the room looked French and a sofa covered in antique blue velvet faced the fireplace. One wall was almost floor-to-ceiling glass and overlooked a fenced yard with neat beds of red roses, a flowering crab apple tree and spirea and hyacinth in bloom. His gaze flicked back to Vivian. Her clothes didn't reveal her figure or her legs, but one of the pictures Thane had carried was of both of them on a beach and Mike had total recall of her long legs and fabulous curves and a smile that could melt ice.

She turned to Mike. "Slade said he's ready, so shall we go? It's a short walk."

"Sure," he said, watching her cross the room and joining her, catching the faintest scent of an exotic perfume. He held the library door for her and then fell into step beside her as they walked down a wide hall that held potted palms and an elegant arrangement of chairs and loveseats. A splashing fountain was built into one of the walls and marble statuary and oils in gilt frames lined each side.

"Is this your art?"

She laughed, a melodic, cheerful sound that made him want to get her to laugh again. "Not all of it. Some of them. I specialize in Western art and portraits. One of the horse paintings is mine." She pointed to the nearest painting. "The black horse."

"Very nice," he said. As he commented, he thought what a pity that Thane's wife wasn't older, less attractive, less appealing and less friendly because then she would definitely be less tempting.

Outside, they followed a stone path bordered by beds of blooming yellow jonquils and purple irises to a gate that he opened and held for her.

"Thank you," she said as she walked through and he followed, closing the gate. "I really know so little about this ranch other than that we raise Hereford cattle. I do ride because we had a family farm that we went to occasionally and I had a horse, but that farm was nothing like this ranch and I didn't spend much time with my horse. And I don't here. I'm really not a ranch person. Also, I think the farm was more of a place for my father to relax."

Mike saw barns, corrals and garages for the various cars, trucks and the one limo. In another direction there were houses and fenced yards. They approached a single-story building with lots of glass and wood.

"Here's the foreman's office. And here comes

Slade," she said as a door opened and a tall, slender man came out. He was in boots, jeans and a long-sleeved denim shirt. In spite of the protection of his broad-brimmed Western hat, his skin was brown, wrinkled and weathered. His gray hair was long at the back of his neck.

"Slade, meet Mike Moretti, Thane's ranger friend. Mike, this is Slade Jackson, our foreman."

As Mike shook hands, he looked into gray eyes that stared intently at him. "I've heard about you from Thane, Mr. Jackson, and what a great job you've always done."

"Call me Slade. Hate to step down, but the time has come. This is a family ranch and it's been here through seven generations of Warners. It goes way back. I understand you've worked on a ranch."

Vivian took a step forward. "Before you answer Slade, I'll tell you two goodbye," she said to the two men. "I enjoyed meeting you, Mike, and we'll talk some more. You and Slade can come to some decisions."

He gazed into her eyes and the thought crossed his mind that he could look at her for hours. Instantly, he thought about her from a few minutes earlier, crying over Thane, the man she once loved. And still loved. Mike knew he hadn't imagined his reaction to touching her and he was equally certain that she had felt something, too. Why did they have the slightest chemistry between them when neither one wanted it? Was it really going to help for him to take her to dinner a couple of times to drive away a bothersome neighbor? Or would an evening together complicate both their lives?

Two

Vivian walked back to the house with her emotions churning. Mike Moretti was the kind of man she had expected from Thane's glowing description. What she hadn't expected was the flash of awareness whenever they made physical contact. They didn't know each other, so it wasn't because she liked him. And she missed Thane every hour of every day. She missed him, she hurt and she didn't want to go out with another man. Asking Mike to take her to dinner had been purely to get Clint to stop bothering her.

She really knew very little about Mike except what Thane had told her. She knew that her new foreman was one of Thane's best buddies. She knew he was single, dependable, trustworthy, honest, strong, intelligent and understood ranching. Thane had mentioned all of those qualities, but as for actual facts about his life, Thane had said almost nothing and she hadn't asked. She had always thought Thane would come home to her and she was still shocked over his death. She hated to ask Mike to take her out, especially on his first day here, but she wanted to be up front about it. She was becoming desperate to get Clint Woodson out of her life. He annoyed her like a fly steadily buzzing around her.

Any of her close friends would know when she went out with Mike that it didn't really mean a thing to her. Clint, however, wouldn't know that. She looked forward to the day when he was no longer bothering her and trying to get her to sell the ranch.

Her thoughts jumped back to Mike and her reaction to shaking his hand this morning. That stirring of awareness, that skitter up her spine, had shocked her and she couldn't get it out of mind. She didn't want to feel anything toward any other man. She loved her husband even if he wasn't coming home to her. Was she making a mistake by going out with Mike?

She told herself she wasn't. After all, she wasn't interested in anything romantic and he didn't act as if he was, either. She shrugged away her worries about going out with him, telling herself it would only be a polite evening with talk about the ranch and maybe good memories from Mike about Thane.

She entered her house and went to her room to change her clothes so she could paint. She didn't expect to see Mike Moretti again until he moved in and worked for the Tumbling T.

Tuesday morning, Slade was showing Mike around the ranch. Everything was in good shape, even the garages where they stopped in for a tour of the vehicles.

Mike turned when Slade held out a set of keys to him.

"Thane wanted you to have his horse and his saddle and his truck." Slade pointed out the newer vehicle to their right. "She's all yours."

"I think that'll do nicely," Mike said, shaking his head and silently thanking his friend. Leave it to Thane to have thought of everything.

After he looked over the truck, he turned to the foreman. "Looks like the Tumbling T is top notch. Is there anything this ranch needs that it doesn't have?"

Slade laughed. "Just an owner. Vivian really doesn't have her heart in this. She likes it out here, but she has no love for ranching, the horses, the land, not even that monster house he had built for her."

Mike smiled. "It is a monster house. At least some people are living in it and enjoying it."

"Yeah, they are. I think they like it more than she does."

The two men walked over to the barn for a tour.

"Wait here and I'll go get Thane's horse," Slade told him. "I can tell you that you're going to like him. He's a winner."

Slade disappeared inside and came back out leading a black horse. Mike's gaze ran over the horse and he smiled. "That is one fine horse."

"He's the best cutting horse on the place. He's fast, fast enough to race. He's the best and Thane loved him. Thane's saddle has his initials on it and it's the fanciest saddle in there. He has more than one, but you'll see the one I'm talking about and you'll like it."

Mike led the horse into a corral and turned him loose, running his hands along his neck, feeling the muscles and the smooth hide, his coarse black mane.

"I think he's waiting for something."

"He likes apples," Slade said.

"I'll remember that next time I see him."

He left, closing the gate and joining Slade on the remainder of the tour.

By the time Mike made it back to the guesthouse that night, he was ready to have a hot shower and to sit and think about all he had learned and seen of the ranch and the people he had met that day. It was dark when he finished his shower. He pulled on jeans and boots and a T-shirt, going outside to sit in a rocker and drink a beer. The guesthouse had a fenced yard and faced the back of the main house where a few lights burned on different floors. He wondered where Vivian's room was and what she was doing.

His eyes had adjusted to the dark and there was a lamp post with a light in the yard, one beyond it near the drive and one farther down along the ranch road. Houses were scattered around him and they all had yard lights. There was a big mulberry tree in the guesthouse yard with lights and there was a white picket fence around the yard. He saw something moving along the outside of the fence and realized it was a shaggy brown dog. Curious, he watched as the dog went to the gate, stood on its hind legs and opened the latch with its nose. It nudged the gate open, came inside and up to the porch, walking up to Mike with a wagging tail.

Mike had to laugh as he scratched the dog's ears. "Smart fella. That deserves a treat, but I don't have one tonight. I'll get one, though, because I suspect you'll be back. Were you Thane's dog or are you the ranch dog and get scratches from everyone?"

As he petted the dog, it raised its head and wagged its tail faster. Out of the corner of his eye, Mike saw someone approaching. "We're going to have company."

The dog left him, trotting to the gate and wagging its tail expectantly.

"Mike?"

He stood as Vivian came through the gate. "Hey, if you wanted to see me, you could have called and I would have come by the house. Next time, send a text."

"No. I was out walking and saw your light, so I thought I'd see if the guesthouse was okay."

He smiled. "It's more than okay. It's a fully furnished house with two bedrooms, two and a half baths and a game room. And a dog must come with it because he knows how to open the gate. Come sit. Want a beer or pop or water or anything?"

"No, thanks. The dog is Sandy. He was Thane's dog, but he's friendly and likes everyone and everyone likes him, so he makes the rounds. Since Thane left, Sandy really prefers staying with Slade. Unless you object, when Slade leaves, I think you'll have a dog."

"That's fine with me. This is a smart dog. Sandy opened the gate with ease."

"Oh, yes. Sandy can open most of the gates, most of the doors. That dog really loved Thane. I think he likes you," she said, looking at the dog standing beside Mike while he scratched Sandy's back.

She sat beside him and he caught a whiff of perfume that smelled like wildflowers and he remembered her soft hand in his when he met her.

"I saw Thane's horse that Slade said is now mine. Also his truck and his saddle."

"They're yours if you want them."

"That's a magnificent horse, the best of saddles and a new truck—of course I'd like them. Thank you."

"Thane told Slade what to do with his things. He tried to take care of all of us."

Mike thought of the packet of money Thane had left him. "That he did. He left me some money, which I put in the bank."

"Whatever he gave you, he wanted you to have, so take it and enjoy it. I will treasure my diamond pendant always. I'm wearing it now."

"I understand. I saw the horses Leon is trying to

gentle and I've met Leon. He looked less than happy to meet me."

"I think he's out of my life. I shouldn't have even told you about him."

"Oh, yes, you should have. Whatever happens on the ranch, I should know about. At least that kind of thing." He sipped his beer and they sat in silence. He looked at the main house with bright lights still on in a few windows. "Is your room on this side of the house?"

"Yes, as a matter of fact. It's on the second floor in the corner. I have a suite and there are windows all along the back. I have that balcony," she said, pointing up at the mansion. "I have one light on in my study there, see? I have a small studio there, too. I'll show you sometime soon."

His eyes followed in the direction she pointed "When you sit on your balcony and I sit out here, I can wave to you and you'll see me?"

"That's right."

"Interesting. Vivian, that house seems big by anyone's standards. Did Thane want a giant home or did you?"

"Thane gave it to me as a gift. Actually, it's way too big. We wanted to have a family but... Well, at least there are employees who live in it."

"So that wasn't your idea."

"Heavens, no. I wanted a studio where I could paint. I wanted a place to hang my finished artwork. I don't know what he had in mind. He had a lot of company and thought we'd have family. Well, that didn't work out, so I've got this mansion to rattle around in." Her voice was quiet and Mike had to admit it was nice to have her there.

Sandy sat at his side while he continued to scratch his head and Mike felt a streak of guilt. Thane should be home with her, sitting beside her on a nice spring night, before going to bed with his wife. Mike pulled his thoughts from that.

"Do you walk often in the evening?" he finally asked her.

"Not really. Thane and I did, but I don't by myself. It was a pretty night and I thought I'd see if you needed anything. It's dark now and I think I'll go back."

He stood. "I'll walk with you."

She smiled. "You don't have to. There's plenty of light."

"I don't mind. I'll get to know the boss."

She nodded, accepting his company as he fell in step beside her, Sandy following them. At the porch steps he took her arm and heard her quick intake of breath and felt a tingle at the contact. As soon as she was off the steps, he released her arm.

They walked across the yard and Mike held the gate. He was aware of Vivian at his side and he wondered if she was lonesome or had simply come to see if he needed anything as she had said.

"Do you miss Dallas?" he asked her.

"Not really. I loved it here when Thane was home. Honestly, it's empty and lonely now. I'd be just as lonely in Dallas, maybe more so. I have a condo there, but I can't see living in it all the time and I don't paint there. This has become home."

When they reached her yard, he held the gate open and they walked up to the patio where she turned to him. "Thanks for walking me home. Now you can take Sandy back with you. Sandy doesn't ever stay with me. He's a man's dog."

"If I don't see you sooner, I'll see you next Friday night at the charity dinner."

"Mike, thanks for agreeing to go with me. I really appreciate it."

"I don't think it's going to be a difficult task," he said with a grin and she laughed.

"I hope not."

"C'mon, Sandy," he said, turning, and the dog walked beside him to the gate where Mike stopped and waved to her because she still stood on the porch watching them.

When she went inside, he looked down at the dog. "What a job this is going to be, boy. You and I both have lost the anchor in our lives—the boss I thought I'd work with for years and your owner. But don't get attached to me, dog," he warned. "I'll be gone in three months."

The first Friday that Mike Moretti was in her employ, late in the afternoon, Vivian heard a motor and glanced out of her studio window to see Mike get out of a pickup, toss his hat in the window and head to the back door. He'd made an appointment to see her and she went to the door to greet him.

"Hi. You look as if you've had a hard day's work," she said, wondering what he had done because he was muddy and they hadn't had any rain. His black hair was tousled. She couldn't control the jump in her heartbeat at the sight of him and figured it was because she hadn't seen any male except Henry for the past week as she'd been holed up in the house painting.

"Sorry, I didn't stop to clean up first. We had a water leak and we'll need to replace a waterline." He glanced down at his muddy clothes and shrugged. "Didn't want to be late for our appointment. I wanted to report in about my first week."

"Want a cold drink—pop, tea, beer? Francie baked cookies, or I have some chips and salsa and we can sit on the patio."

"Only if I can clean up a little first."

"Of course you can. C'mon. I'll show you. Henry is around some place, but he's getting ready to go out tonight." She led him through the entryway and pointed to an open door. "There's a bathroom and I'll be in the kitchen. When you come out, go straight ahead and turn left at the first door."

She went to the kitchen where Francie was putting away the last of some clean dishes from the dishwasher. The tall red-haired cook smiled at Vivian. "I was finishing up before I leave. I put the last batch of cookies on that platter and the others are in the cookie jar. Your dinner is cooked and all you'll have to do is reheat it in the microwave. There's a roast that's done and in the fridge for the weekend, plus other food."

"Thank you. Mike Moretti is here. He's the man who will replace Slade. I came to get him a beer and myself a glass of water. I don't think he'll want cookies with his beer, but I'll take the platter to the patio, plus some chips and salsa."

"I have a batch of homemade salsa I can take out and—" She stopped and smiled. Vivian glanced around as Mike entered the kitchen.

"Mike, meet Francie Ellison. Francie, this is Mike Moretti."

"Call me Mike," he said. "That's easier." They smiled at each other.

"Glad to meet you, Mike. I'm leaving, but I'll take these chips and salsa to the patio."

"I'll carry them," he said, taking them from her hands. "Now you can start your weekend off."

"Thanks. Welcome to the Tumbling T. Do you need anything else before I go?" she asked Vivian, who shook her head as she opened a beer for Mike and then got a tray for everything they would take outside.

"No, thanks. You have a nice weekend and I'll see you Monday.

She was aware of her old jeans, faded red T-shirt and bare feet. She resisted the urge to smooth down her hair, which was pulled back in a thick braid, and instead, led Mike outside.

"It's been a busy week and a good one getting to

know everyone," he said once they were seated and he'd taken a draft of his beer. "I'll miss Slade because he's a nice guy, but I'm happy for him to get to retire and it sounds as if he needs to."

"He definitely needs to. The last time he was home, Thane said Slade should have retired a couple of years ago. Thane thought it might have saved him so much back trouble." She took a sip of her cold water. "I hope you like the job. I'm sure Slade hopes you do, too."

Mike nodded. "It's a good job. I can see Thane's touch in things all around the ranch." He put his beer on the table and sat back on the cushioned chair. "I told you when I came that I'm muddy because we had a water pipe spring a leak. A long stretch will have to be replaced."

As they talked, she gazed into his green eyes and became so lost in them, she barely heard what he was saying. Why did she have this keen awareness of him? Was it purely the absence of a man in her life? She didn't think so. She was surrounded by men on the ranch. Henry, the staff that worked in the house and in the yard, the cowboys that she saw when she went to the garage or one of the barns. It went beyond a keen awareness and no matter how much she wanted to ignore it, she had to admit it was there. She was attracted to Mike and she knew he felt something, too. She didn't want that attraction to him and she suspected he didn't want to feel it, either.

Right now, she was acutely aware of him. Looking into his thickly lashed green eyes made her heart race. He was tall, broad-shouldered, good-looking. Maybe too good-looking, an inner voice told her. How difficult was it going to be to go to a charity ball with him next weekend? The thought of stepping into his arms to dance made her tingle from head-to-toe.

She had talked to Slade about Mike and the old foreman was as enthused about him as Thane had been, which was a relief but not a surprise. Slade was ready to step down and let Mike take over. With Slade retiring in south Texas where his son and oldest daughter lived, her life was changing again. Slade and Thane had been a big part of her life for the past year and soon they would both be gone. But Mike Moretti would not be in her life as much as Slade had been.

She didn't expect to see much of Mike when he took over. First of all, he was new to the job so she expected him to be at work most of the time when he was on the ranch. He would report during the week via emails and texts. Slade always had come by at least once a week to talk to her about the ranch and she expected him to tell Mike to do the same.

Why did the prospect of seeing him at least once a week excite her?

And why was Mike looking at her now as if he expected her to reply?

"I'm sorry," she said, forcing her thoughts back to the conversation. "What were you saying?"

"I said you're from Dallas, right? I mean, I really

don't know anything about you except that you were Thane's wife and happily married."

"Happily married and married too short of a time," she said. "Sorry. I miss him. We used to sit out here and talk at night when he came in off the ranch."

"He was a really good guy."

"That's high praise. He thought you were, too. He always said he could count on you to come through."

Mike looked across the yard as if looking far away from the ranch. "I didn't come through at the last. I tried, but I couldn't save him."

"Don't take any blame there. Neither could the doctors at the hospital. A chaplain wrote to me that Thane was picked up by a helicopter and taken to a field hospital. He died when they were transferring him to the hospital."

They were both silent a moment. "You came through, Mike. You tried to save him, but they wrote he was too badly injured. You got all his last messages and what he wanted you to take home. That gave him some peace, I'm sure."

Mike turned to focus on her and another tingle tickled her. "I don't know much about you except what I've seen in Dallas papers about your dad. I know more about him and his success in the hotel business. You have a brother-in-law who helps your dad run that business now, don't you? And your brother runs the oil business."

"Yes. My brother-in-law Sam is good at what he

does. He's married to my older sister, Natalie. They have two cute kids, Holly and Fletcher. Holly is eight and Fletcher is six. I miss them, but they're in school and even if I were back in Dallas I wouldn't see them much."

"Where did you meet Thane?"

"He was good friends with Phil, my older brother. This was the Warner family ranch, but Thane's folks had a home in Dallas, too. His dad never much liked the ranch, but when Thane graduated from college, he came here to take over from his grandfather. His dad never really came back to the ranch. The oil company in Dallas was his love."

"So you knew Thane a long time," he said, looking at her. Just a glance was like a physical contact and she couldn't understand the volatile reaction she had to simply sitting with and talking to him. He was polite, even a little remote. While he was friendly, she had a feeling he had a lot bottled up inside that he didn't talk about.

"That's right. Phil and Thane were friends all through school. Thane was six years older than I am. It made a difference when I was in school. It didn't later."

"Clint Woodson wasn't around much until Thane left, right? I mean, Thane never even mentioned his neighbor."

"That's right. I barely knew who he was until Thane deployed. And like I said, I didn't let Thane know what a pest Clint has been. I didn't want to worry him when he was so far from home. He couldn't do anything about Clint."

"He could have asked some guys here to be a buffer to keep him from disturbing you."

"I was afraid he would ask Slade and Slade has all he can handle."

Mike nodded. As he sipped his beer and looked at the yard, her gaze ran over him. She guessed he was several inches over six feet. He had a narrow waist and long legs. He had one booted foot on his knee and he looked completely relaxed. With the physical awareness she had of him—she was certain it was mutual—was she asking for more trouble by going to the club with him next weekend?

He had been nothing but polite toward her, yet she knew he felt something, too. That made her doubly aware of him. At least, in Mike's case, his reactions seemed unwanted. He seemed to have no personal interest in her and she was glad. She hurt over her loss of the man she loved and she didn't want anyone else in her life yet.

"I hope we're doing the right thing by going to the club Friday night."

He misinterpreted her meaning, and she let him. "It won't hurt to let him think there's a man in your life now. Besides, it's an evening out," he said, smiling at her.

Maybe, she thought, but it wasn't an ordinary evening out. Not when her skin sizzled at his smile.

"I hope Clint is there Friday night. The tickets

were bought in my name, so he can find out if I plan to attend."

"If I had to bet, from what you've told me, I'd put money on your neighbor being there Friday night." He finished off his beer then stood. "I should get going now, Vivian." When he simply said her name, she felt another ripple of attraction.

He began to pick up the dishes but she stopped him. "Leave everything, Mike," she said. "I can carry that stuff to the kitchen."

"So can I," he said and left with everything on the tray except her glass of water. She waited until he returned.

"Thanks for coming to work at the Tumbling T Ranch."

"I promised Thane I would. I'm keeping that promise. If it's a quiet weekend, I won't even come by Monday morning. I can send you a text."

"Thanks. Be sure to make a list of what you want done to Slade's house and when he leaves, we can be ready to get a crew started making changes."

"Sure. I travel lightly, as I said before, and all I need is a bed at night, so I don't think I'll have many changes. Thanks for the beer and I'll see you next week," he said and turned to walk away in long purposeful strides.

She watched him get in his pickup and drive away without looking back.

He said he traveled light and there was no woman in his life to mind if he took her out Friday night.

Thane and Slade thought he was a great guy. Other than that, she knew nothing about him. She had a feeling she would have to depend on him for a lot of things concerning the ranch. She had with Slade, but that had been different, she admitted.

She pulled the diamond pendant Thane had sent home from under her red T-shirt and rolled the diamond between her fingers while she thought about Mike. She added one more item to the list of what she knew about the man: She had an electrifying reaction to him.

"Thane, sweetie, why did you hire Mike and send him here?" she sighed. "I have a feeling he's going to complicate my life."

Mike stepped back and watched the foal stand on its wobbly legs. "She's a little beauty," he said.

"She is," Slade agreed. "Her mama's one of our best mares. The foal is perfect and you did a good, efficient delivery job here, Mike, but I knew you would. Thane really had faith in you."

Mike smiled. "I'm beginning to think Thane laid it on a little thick when he told all of you about me. And I think the mama gets credit for her baby coming easily into the world."

Slade shook his head. "Nope. Thane wouldn't exaggerate. I don't worry about leaving here now." He regarded the newborn foal more closely then turned to Mike. "You know, I worked for Thane's grandfather actually, so I've been here a long time and I can tell you, you'll like it here. This is a good place and you'll get to run it like it's your own ranch, at least until she marries again or sells the place. The hermit life she leads isn't going to get her married, though. She's had a rough time over losing Thane."

"That part about running this place the way I want sounds good," Mike said. "But in my experience, there's always something you didn't count on happening and it throws you."

"That's life, but I'm relieved you're here to handle it so I can get out of here a little sooner. I've worked hard all my life. Mike, I'm seventy-eight and I'm ready to retire and I've got a back problem that driving a pickup over rough ground or sitting in a saddle or a thousand other things around here aggravates. I want to sit under the shade of a tree with a cold beer and enjoy my grandkids."

Mike clapped the man on his shoulder. "I hope you get to do that for a long time, Slade. This is a good ranch and I'm glad to have a job here." He bent down to pick up his delivery instruments from the hay-covered floor. "Mrs. Warner doesn't seem to take much interest in it, though."

"She doesn't know anything about ranching and I don't think she cares. I doubt she'll stay. She liked it out here fine enough when her husband was alive but now… Well, I think she stays because it's peaceful for her and she can paint and she goes to Santa Fe and Houston and other places with her art. She won't interfere with you. As far as daily living, this ranch might as well belong to me and it might as well belong to you when I leave. You'll have free rein to run it the way you want. There are good weeks like this past one and then there are times when you think everything has gone to hell. Fires, bad weather, drought, but you've been in worse situations where men around you died, so this probably looks pretty good."

Mike stood up. "It looks damn good."

Slade nodded. "I figured since you were buddies with Thane and he thought you were such a great rancher that you might be more likely to want your own spread."

"Nope. I don't come from money," Mike said. "Far from it. This job is better than what I expected to begin with when I got home. If Mrs. Warner sells the place and I don't like the new boss, I can move on to another job."

"Frankly, I was glad to hear you weren't getting your own place. I was surprised, though, because I wondered how long you'd work for someone else. I thought maybe you were doing this to get some experience."

Mike shook his head. "I'm doing it because I get paid to do it." He didn't tell Slade about his promise to Thane.

"I can relate to that," Slade said, pushing off from the stall gate. "Best be going now, son. Mrs. Warner told me she asked you to take her out because of that damn Woodson. I think that will run him off fast.

You go get cleaned up. This little baby looks fine and dandy." They both looked at the foal, its spindly long legs already steadier.

"She's beautiful," Mike said. "So is her mama." He finished gathering up his things and placed them in the box in the back of his pickup.

Mike climbed into the truck, waved and drove away, heading back to the guesthouse to get ready for his first date with Vivian Warner.

He only wished he was looking forward to it as much as Slade seemed to be. Mike hoped one date would be enough to divert Clint Woodson's attention from the beautiful widow.

Not to mention his own.

An hour later, Mike left the guesthouse and drove his pickup down the road to the main house. A white limo was parked in the carport at the side of the house.

He was with Slade every day and Slade sent reports to Vivian, but other than a text Monday morning and their chat last Friday afternoon, Mike hadn't talked to her since he was hired on. She seemed to have an even smaller part in the ranch than Thane had led him to believe. Slade hadn't said yet when he would hand in his resignation and Mike didn't ask questions. He liked it here, liked the work, the feel of the dirt under his boots, the people. If Thane had been able to come home, the job would have been perfect.

Mike wondered what the evening ahead would be like. Whether it'd be as awkward as he predicted, his being in a fancy club among rich folk. Mike never forgot his status in life and Vivian's: a cowboy and a billionaire heiress.

He wondered if Clint Woodson would accept that Vivian was going out with her future foreman. Mike hoped he did so this charade would end quickly.

Vivian didn't seem bothered by the monetary difference in their lives, but she knew full well that he worked for her and she was worth billions more than he was. Heck, she was buying his dinner tonight and it bothered him slightly. Even though they were a low income family, his dad had instilled a strong sense that a man should pay. He had always said to Mike and his brothers, "Never take money from a woman. It's a man's place to pay, not the woman. It doesn't work out well if a man marries a woman with way more money than he has. Look at your uncle." Mike's uncle had had a messy divorce from a wealthy woman with lots of ill feelings between the families afterward.

Growing up, Mike had heard plenty about the man paying the woman's way and it was ingrained into him to the point it didn't matter what Vivian thought. He had always agreed with his dad on the topic. It seemed right for the man to pay. He had known some low-life guys in college who let the woman always pay and that hadn't impressed him, Even when his dad died and times got really tough, he still grew up following his dad's teachings. In high school there were times he went hungry before he'd let a woman pay. There was an older teacher who knew his circumstances at home the year his dad died, and she would try to buy his lunch occasionally, He always turned her down even if it meant going hungry. When he rang the bell at the mansion, Henry opened the door. The butler/bodyguard was in a white shirt, a tan sports jacket and dark brown slacks. His collar was unbuttoned.

"Come in, Mike," Henry said, stepping back to hold the door and then closed it behind Mike. "Vivian is waiting. She told me she asked you to take her out. I'm glad. I've never trusted Clint." He held out a small slip of paper, which Mike took. "Here's my cell phone number. My wife and I are going to dinner in Dallas with your driver Ben and his wife." He explained that after Ben dropped them off at the charity ball he was meeting them at a restaurant in town. "But we won't be far should you need the limo or us for any reason," he added.

"Have you ever had trouble with Clint Woodson?"

Henry shook his head. "No, I haven't. He doesn't look the type to cause real trouble, but I promised Thane I'd watch out for Vivian and I'm keeping that promise even though you're with her."

"Thanks." Mike looked down at Henry's cell phone number and memorized it. Then he put the paper in his jacket pocket. "We won't be out late."

"Do what you want. I figure you can take care of

yourself. We shouldn't have any trouble, but I'm not taking a chance. This guy has been obnoxious when he thought she was alone, but I think he'll stop trying to see her now that you're here. Slade couldn't deal with him. You can, and he'll know it the minute he sees you. And if he thinks Vivian wants to go out with you, the man should be smart enough to leave you alone. Every guy on this ranch knows you were a US Army Ranger and that means everyone in the county that has any interest in this ranch knows you were a ranger. Just like they all know I was a marine. That includes Clint. He isn't going to aggravate you."

"I don't think he will, either."

"I just want to be around if we're needed." He motioned Mike down the hall. "Vivian is in the study. I'll show you where."

"No need. I remember," Mike said, moving past Henry. He walked down the hall, turned a corner into the main hall and walked to the open study door. Knocking on the open door, he glanced around the room and saw Vivian by a window. He inhaled deeply, his gaze riveted on her as she turned and smiled at him.

She wore a sleeveless red gown of some soft material that clung to her curvy body and revealed her slender figure and tiny waist. In the low-cut V-neckline, the diamond pendant from Thane sparkled. With that one glance, all Mike's peace of mind over the past few days shattered. He thought he would remember how she looked in this moment for the rest of his life.

"You're gorgeous," he said as she walked up. He realized what he had said to her and hurried to correct himself. "I'm sorry, I know we should keep this evening impersonal."

Her melodic laugh eased the tension he felt. "Don't worry, Mike. Thane is gone and he wouldn't be angry if you complimented me, anyway. A compliment is welcome, especially from a good-looking guy, so don't apologize. We're friends, or I hope we will be, because right now we barely know each other. A compliment between friends is always welcome."

He relaxed a fraction, relieved that she had taken his admiration lightly and could laugh about it. Laughter, however, wasn't what he was feeling. He couldn't stop looking at her. She was so stunning that his heart was racing. He didn't want that kind of reaction when looking at his friend's wife. He felt an obligation to Thane to keep a distance from Vivian. It didn't matter that much that she was a widow. He felt honor bound to keep his distance. Thane didn't hire him to come home and seduce his wife.

All evening he would be with Thane's gorgeous, breathtaking wife who made his pulse pound and heated the room another ten degrees by being there. And he would have to relax and look as if he was enjoying himself or Clint Woodson would never be fooled.

Could he do that?

Before he could answer, Vivian's question broke into his thoughts. "The limo is ready, so shall we go?" she asked.

"Sure," he said, walking beside her, but taking care to leave space between them. "Your necklace is beautiful. Thane chose well," he said, thinking more about her than the necklace.

She touched it with perfectly manicured red fingernails. "I will always treasure this. I don't expect to ever marry again. Thane was the love of my life even though we didn't have much time together."

"You'll marry again," Mike said, unable to keep from smiling at her.

"I'm not going to argue that point tonight. I'm happy to go out, and I think this will stop Clint from pestering me and that's an enormous relief."

"You could have found some cowboy on the ranch to do what I'm doing."

She shook her head. "Clint would never have believed that I was doing anything except trying to avoid him. It wouldn't have stopped him. This, however, most likely will stop him. You're an unknown factor and you're good-looking and—"

"Thank you," he said, nodding at her.

"Well, that's a fact. But you have something about you that says 'don't mess with me.'"

Mike couldn't help the slight chuckle that rose from his chest. "This is going to be an interesting evening. I feel as if I'm going to get my fortune told."

"Don't be ridiculous. I have no idea about your

future. I'm merely an artist and I'm observant and I've painted portraits of scores of people. I'll draw your picture if you want," she said, and he knew she was teasing him.

"Thanks. But you should use your talents on real stuff."

"You're definitely real stuff," she said while he held the door for her. She switched on the alarm and the lock clicked as he closed the door.

"I told Henry that they could ride with us in the limo, but he wanted to drive," she explained as they walked down the path.

"I think Henry half expects there might be trouble from Clint tonight. I thought you said he's never given you any physical threat."

"He hasn't. Henry's afraid he might have some guys come after you."

"I doubt that. It's our first time out and we're at a country club and we're in a limo. I don't think we'll have a problem."

"I don't think so either or I wouldn't go tonight. Clint is a pest, but I don't think he would stoop to anything violent. Or hire anyone to do something bad. I'm going to have a good time tonight. We'll convince Clint that we're attracted to each other. And while we do that, I'll enjoy the evening. Mike, I haven't been out like this in oh, so long."

"Neither have I as a matter of fact. I'm sure we can convince Clint that you have someone in your life now. While we do that, I hope you can have a good time."

They reached the limo and Vivian greeted her driver for the evening then turned back to Mike. "Mike, you probably know Ben."

"I do," he said, looking at the tall cowboy who had changed his jeans and hat and was now wearing black slacks and a white shirt. "We were together about three hours ago. Hi, Ben," Mike said easily, offering his hand to the cowhand.

"Hi. It's going to be a nice night."

"That it is," Mike said.

In seconds they were seated in the limo and Ben went around to the front to drive. Mike sat on the long seat with a lot of space between Vivian and him. He turned slightly to face her.

"So tell me about yourself, Mike," she said. "I don't know anything except Thane trusted you totally and counted you as one of his closest friends."

"We lived in Amarillo," he said, beginning a rote description of his life that he had become so accustomed to giving, he didn't need to think about it. He was light years away from the life she'd had with limos and servants and all kinds of opportunities. "I worked on ranches and went to school on scholarships. I won some money in rodeos. My dad died when I was a teen. I have two older brothers and one younger. With four boys, my mom had a hard time making ends meet, but we all got part-time jobs, scholarships, that sort of thing." He shrugged.

"That's it. Nothing exciting. I'd much rather hear about your background. You told me a little about your family. Where did you go to college?"

"The University of Texas where I majored in art. No surprise there."

"And then you came home to start painting?"

"That's about right. I opened the Dallas gallery the second year I was out of college and I did well those early years, showing my paintings and others."

Mike listened, but he paid more attention to the woman rather than the words. He could sit and look at her all evening. In the dim light of the limo he could see the antique diamond laying against her flawless creamy skin. He took a deep breath and shifted his gaze higher to look into the bluest pair of eyes ever. Vivian looked so breathtaking, that he was grateful there would be a lot of people around tonight, including some friends she had joining them. That would make it a lot easier to keep the conversation impersonal and to keep from flirting with her. The woman was head-to-toe temptation. He hoped they didn't have many of these dinners before Clint Woodson disappeared from her life. It constantly nagged at him that Thane had trusted him to come home to help her not to come home to seduce her.

Lights blazed at the country club as the limo rolled up a wide drive and stopped at the front door. Ben held the door and told Mike to call later when they were ready to be picked up.

Mike took her arm lightly as they walked inside.

The minute he touched her, he had the same searing awareness that he'd had before. They weren't talking or even looking at each other, yet his skin tingled. Instantly he lowered his arm, banishing the sensation and promising himself he'd avoid further contact. He didn't want to feel that awareness around her.

In the center of the entryway, the round fruitwood table beneath a mammoth chandelier held a large crystal vase of red anthuriums and deep purple gladiolus. Guests and members stood talking to each other while staff hurried around them. Vivian spoke to a maître d' and he looked at his chart.

"Table four, Ray," he said. A waiter in a matching black suit and bow tie with a white shirt hurried over. "Table four," the maître d' repeated as Ray gathered menus and smiled at them.

"Good evening, Mrs. Warner. Sir, if you'll please follow me, I'll show you to your table."

As they followed the waiter in single file past the tables, Mike glanced briefly at the sway of Vivian's hips. With an effort, he turned his attention to the room around him. It was an older club with polished oak floors, ornate crystal chandeliers and thick blue carpet that muffled the noise. A piano player sat in a corner playing old ballads and there was a hum of conversation. Each table was centered with a vase of fresh pink roses and daisies.

As soon as they were seated, she received a text. "My friends are about fifteen minutes away so they'll be here soon."

"This is a big crowd."

"Which means they raised a lot of money for Parkinson's disease. Oh, oh," she said. "I think you're about to meet Clint. Mike," she said, her voice lowering to a whisper, "please take my hand so it looks as if this is more than a friendly dinner."

"Vivian, look at me and forget him. He'll have to interrupt us if he wants to talk to us. Frankly, I want to meet him. It's best to know your enemy. Surprises aren't good."

As she instructed, he reached over to take her hand in his. Her fingers were cool from touching the goblet of ice water, but at the contact, heat flashed within him as quick as lightning. He gazed into her blue eyes and the dining room grew instantly warmer and he bit back several things that he would like to say but knew better not to.

Damn. He'd resolved not to touch her, yet here he was, only minutes later, holding her hand.

And now he was paying the price.

Three

"Good evening, Vivian."

At the sound of the man's voice, at first Mike was filled with trepidation at meeting Vivian's pushy neighbor, yet relieved to finally let go of her hand. He stood and held out his hand to shake the rancher's as Vivian introduced them.

"Clint, this is Mike Moretti, Thane's friend and my new foreman," she said without hesitation.

"New foreman? That's a good job," Clint remarked as he scanned Mike with a rake of his eyes. Mike felt as if he was being measured and dismissed. Clint eventually shook his hand, and Mike looked into cold hazel eyes. Broad-shouldered, Clint was as tall as Mike and handsome enough for some women to find him appealing. He had thick black hair with a few curls above his forehead. His clothes looked expensive as did the gold rings he wore on several fingers.

"I heard Thane hired you when you both were in the service," Clint said to Mike.

"That's right."

"Have you ever been a foreman before this job? That's a big job."

"Yes, it is, and the Tumbling T is a fine ranch. And yes, I was a foreman before." He wasn't about to give Clint Woodson any details of his life, but he had been a foreman on a Texas ranch for two years before he joined the Army.

"We're neighbors, in case you didn't know."

"That's what Vivian told me."

Woodson gave him another once-over, then clearly he'd seen enough. "I'll see you around." And without waiting for Mike's reply, he promptly turned his back on Mike and focused solely on Vivian. "How're you tonight?"

Mike sat down again and sipped his water while he listened to Clint talk to Vivian. "I have a new proposition I'd like to talk to you about sometime soon. I think it would be mutually beneficial to both ranches since we're in a drought."

"Maybe you can run it past Mike," Vivian replied. "Right now, I think we're doing fine, and it's April. Texas usually has spring rains."

"Yes, well, you have a good evening, Vivian," he said, leaning down slightly and speaking softly.

"I'll see you around." He walked away without even glancing back at Mike.

"So now you know Clint Woodson," she said as she resumed her seat at the table.

"So I do." It occurred to him he hadn't updated Vivian on the Clint situation, so he took the opportunity. "I've already talked to Slade about keeping a man at the front gate and he's agreeable to it. Is there anywhere else Clint might enter the ranch?"

"No. There's another way in, but that gate is locked and only certain people on the ranch have keys or know the code to get in."

"Yeah, Slade showed that gate to me. I wondered if there's anywhere else you know about but Slade doesn't."

She shook her head. "But we're neighbors, so all he has to do is get over the fence that divides the two ranches. He can't drive in and Clint would never climb a fence and walk across the ranch to the house." She cast a glance over her shoulder to the rancher as he walked away, then turned back to Mike. "Thanks, Mike, for taking my hand when he approached. Clint saw that. He didn't like it and he didn't like you."

Mike looked across the room and saw Clint sit at a table. The woman sitting there turned to greet him. She was a head-turner with black hair in an elaborate upsweep and a black dress that clung to her slim silhouette. Even from this vantage point, Mike could see the tight skirt of the dress was slit clear up to her thigh. "He's here with a friend."

"That's Dora Grayson. She has her own real estate agency in Dallas. A very successful woman." Vivian smiled, her tight voice relaxing as she said, "Here are my friends."

Mike stood and turned, looking at a couple approaching their table. The top of the woman's head barely reached her companion's shoulder and her light brown eyes sparkled with friendliness.

Vivian made the introductions. "Ashlynn and Dan, this is Mike Moretti. Mike, meet my childhood friend Ashlynn Coleman and her husband, Dan Coleman."

Dan had a slight beard, high cheekbones and a rugged appearance that was softened when he smiled. His wife was a pretty woman with midnight tresses that fell straight over her shoulders. She wore a deep blue sleeveless gown with a straight skirt that highlighted her slender figure.

Mike received a firm handshake from Dan and Ashlynn gave him a warm smile.

Mike sat between Vivian on his right and Dan on his left. After a few minutes Dan turned to him. "Do you like the ranch?"

"Absolutely. It's up-to-date, a big operation, nice guys, it's great—all Thane said it would be."

"You get rid of Clint Woodson and you'll be the miracle man. Ashlynn and Vivian are close, so Vivian has told her about Clint. There's no love lost between Clint and me, but we stay civil to each other because we're at a lot of the same functions and know the same people due to our connections in the oil business. But I don't like Clint and he doesn't like me."

Mike knew the feeling. "Clint has already stopped to meet me and talk to Vivian. Don't worry. I'll keep him off the ranch."

"Good deal." Dan clapped him on the back. "Enough about that. Do you keep up with baseball?"

"I do since I'm home again." For the next few minutes, Mike talked to Dan about baseball, until their waiter appeared to take their drink orders.

Mike enjoyed her friends and as they went through dinner, he glanced around the room casually, each time catching Clint watching Vivian. Mike knew he should keep his attention on Vivian to convince Clint that he was interested in her. He stopped looking at Clint, focusing on Vivian and giving her his full attention, which was easy to do.

When Dan asked Ashlynn to dance, Mike asked Vivian. He took a deep breath before she stepped into his arms out on the dance floor for a ballad. He held her a discreet distance and she smiled at him, her blue eyes holding mischief.

"Scared to touch me, Mike? I don't think Thane would mind. I think we would be more convincing to Clint that we're interested in each other."

"We probably would convince Clint faster, but there are more reasons than just thinking about Thane," he said, trying to keep his voice light. "For one, you're my boss."

"Ah, the alpha male. I'll bet almost a hundred percent of the Marines, the Airbornes, the US Rangers and all their ilk are alpha males. I guess it goes with the territory."

He smiled and relaxed a fraction as he danced her around. "It does go with the territory and so does flirting with beautiful women and dancing close and hot, steamy kisses. Watch out, boss. I might forget my place."

She laughed and the twinkle was still in her eyes. "Oh, the big strong, handsome man can be— What? Scary? No, I don't think so. Thrilling? Ah, that's the word."

This was a side to Vivian that Mike hadn't yet seen—playful, teasing. Wanting. He wasn't sure how to react to it. "Vivian, you're asking for trouble."

"That means I don't scare you," she said in a sultry voice.

"You scare the hell out of me because I shouldn't like dancing with you. I shouldn't like flirting with you. I shouldn't want to kiss you. I shouldn't feel anything when our fingers touch and neither should you."

"For a US Army Ranger, you're a little stuffy."

He had to grin. "That's a first in my life. I have never been told I'm stuffy. You're going to goad me into doing something about that." He caught her around the waist and took long steps, dancing in circles through the terrace doors and outside on to the patio where it was darker and cooler.

"Try this for stuffy, darlin'." He pulled her tightly against him and kissed her. He knew he shouldn't, but he was having more fun with her than he could recall having had anywhere, anytime in the past three years when he was in the Army.

When did his kiss change from all in fun to something deeper, he wondered. It was as if a golden chain was pulling him down into a raging fire of longing. The feel of her mouth on his was driving every thought out of his mind, burning away everything but desire. He hadn't held a woman in a long time. He hadn't held a woman like her in a lifetime. She was delectable, enticing, voluptuous, her soft curves pressing against him. She smelled wonderful and her skin was smooth, her hair silky.

And she was off-limits.

Yet he couldn't stop kissing her. Kisses to die for. Kisses that burned, scalded and made him want more. She had teased, enticed and maneuvered him into kissing her and now he was going to pay for rising to the challenge.

He swung her up and the look she gave him was serious.

"Get Ben and Henry and let's get out of here now," she whispered.

He didn't ask why they had to rush out, but grabbed his phone and typed a brief text message as they left the patio. She grabbed her purse from the table and hurried out of the ballroom with him.

Only when they were alone in the rotunda did she explain her abrupt action. "When we were…kissing, I saw Clint at the terrace door. He was looking at you and his expression was scary. His face was red and he seemed furious."

Mike let out his breath. "If that's why you're rushing out, relax. We'll leave, but Clint isn't going to do anything crazy to mess up his life. He's got too much to lose. Besides, his anger is directed at only me, not you, I'm sure. I can deal with Clint. So can Henry and Ben. Don't worry." He slipped his arm around her waist and pulled her close against his side. "We have accomplished all you wanted to accomplish tonight. That's what you set out to do—convince Clint there's a man in your life now. I think you succeeded. So smile, Vivian."

"If you say so." Yet no smile tugged at her lips. "I'll text Ashlynn that we're leaving so they don't wonder where we are."

In minutes, he heard her phone and she looked at her message. "Ashlynn and Dan are headed to the front to get their car. They're ready to go home, too."

As they walked to the front entrance, Mike looked down at her and she gazed up at him with a long, searching look. "You're really not worried about Clint, are you?"

"No, I'm not. He's not the type for violence. That would destroy what he wants. He's just angry because a guy beat him to winning you over—or so he thinks. You did exactly what you hoped to do tonight. And then some. But, Vivian, don't pressure me into doing things I shouldn't do."

Suddenly, she smiled and he thought it was like discovering a rainbow in a gray sky. Everything was bright and beautiful again.

"If you think you shouldn't have kissed me," she said softly, "you're wrong."

He dropped his arm from her waist. "You're off-limits. Totally. For a moment, I forgot that."

She stepped closer and shook her head. "I'm not 'off-limits,' cowboy. I'm a lonely widow who hasn't been out dancing in over a year. We kissed. One kiss. That's not a life-changing big deal."

"Well, thank you, darlin'," he said, unable to keep from laughing.

"Aha, see! You know you're being ridiculous. It was a fun moment and I have had damn few of them since my husband deployed."

He imagined she likely hadn't. So he smiled at her and didn't argue the point. He took her arm. "C'mon. Ben and Henry are going to come charging in here any minute now because of my terse message. They'll think I'm getting beaten to a pulp or some such."

They stepped outside where they saw Henry and Ben standing by the limo.

In seconds, they reached the limo. "We're fine," Mike said. "Just crossed signals. Hope we didn't cut the night short for all of you."

"We're here to serve," Henry said lightly. "We're fine. It's a long drive back to the ranch anyway. If you don't mind, Ben's wife will ride up front with him."

He didn't wait for Vivian's opinion. "No, we don't mind," he answered for both of them. "You'll be

happy to know that I think we accomplished our purpose with Clint tonight, so it's time to go."

Henry gave him a thumbs-up as Ben held open
the limo door.

Mike still left a lot of space between Vivian and
him in the back seat.

"Scared to sit close to me?" she asked.

He looked up at her, able to see her clearly even in
the dim interior lighting. He couldn't stop the hon-
esty in his response. "Yes. As I said, Vivian, you
are off-limits."

He heard her long sigh. "Well, for a little while
there, you were fun, and I had fun," she said with a
forlorn note in her voice.

It tore at him. At this moment the one thing he
wanted most in the world was to take her in his
arms and kiss her for the next few hours. He scooted
close and drew her against his side, slipping his arm
around her and holding her. "Is that better?"

"Yes, it is," she answered and her voice sounded
solemn.

"I did have fun, Vivian," he said in a somber tone.
"But I wouldn't be doing right by Thane if I came
home and did anything to cause you harm. I also
don't want to lose a very good job. Surely you can
understand that." He said the words to Vivian but he
wondered whether he was really trying to convince
himself. One thing he was sure of—he wasn't ever
going to forget kissing her tonight. That had been the
hottest, most luscious, exciting kiss of his life. Could

he go home tonight and forget he kissed her? A bigger question—could he resist ever doing it again?

Henry dropped them off at Vivian's where Mike had his pickup parked. As he walked across the porch seeing her to the door, she surprised him with an invitation. "Come in for a while, Mike. It's still early in the evening."

He shook his head. "It's been a fun, interesting night, Vivian, but I'm going home now before I do something I shouldn't."

"Is it because you still see me as Thane's wife?"

"That's part of it," he answered truthfully. Only a small part. He felt torn in two now because half of him wanted badly to stay, but the other half of him knew if he did, he wouldn't be able to keep from kissing her again. It was safer, smarter, better to go back to his place.

"So what's the other part?"

"I think we might complicate each other's lives."

"You don't want to come in because I'm your boss. That's it, isn't it?" she asked, sounding disapproving. "You're incredibly old-fashioned."

"I might be," he said, "but I'm not going to let you provoke me into losing my control for the second time tonight." He backed up. "I'll see you Monday morning."

He hadn't taken two steps off the porch when he heard her again.

"Mike, it was a terrific night and it was great to

be able to forget heartache, loss and grief for a short time. Thanks."

He stood with his back to her, breathing deeply, torn between wanting to go back and kiss her or doing what he knew he should do and get in his pickup and go. He turned around to look at her. She stood in the light from the porch and she looked so forlorn, his heart actually ached for her. "Damn," he whispered so softly she couldn't possibly have heard him.

He walked back to her, stopping about a foot away.

"Vivian, I'm not going to come home and make love to my friend's wife."

"Thane's gone out of my life, Mike. And it was just a kiss. For a few minutes tonight, life was happy again."

He sighed and closed the distance between them, taking her in his arms and kissing her again. Once he made the decision, he threw aside his reluctance, his guilt, his good sense to keep his distance. He threw himself into another impassioned kiss, holding her tightly against him as he leaned over her while his tongue stroked hers.

She wrapped her arms around him, her fingers winding in his short hair at the back of his head. He groaned. She was soft, passionate, sensuous, and she was making him hot and hard. More than anything he wanted to carry her off to bed—but that was a line he wouldn't cross.

He ran his hand down her back, over the fullness of her bottom, down to the split in her dress to push it open and caress her warm thigh. He was on fire, yet at the same time trembling while he hung on to his control to not go any further.

He swung her up, gazing into her eyes. "You're going to get yourself into trouble, Vivian."

"I feel as if you're bringing me to life again, bringing me back into a world of passion and joy. I've had a wonderful time."

He released her and stepped back. "I'm glad, Vivian. But I have to go now."

"I'm glad you came back," she said softly.

"So am I," he said, smiling at her. With an effort he turned away to walk to his pickup. He drove back to the guesthouse. Only when he saw in the rearview mirror that she had gone inside and closed the door did he fully let out his breath. He ached and he wanted her and he wondered if he would want her for the rest of his life.

But Vivian Warner was off-limits to him. He didn't want to be dazzled, set on fire with scorching desire by a woman who was his deceased buddy's wife, a billion-dollar heiress and his boss to boot. But how was he going to resist such an incredibly sexy, desirable woman? How would he ever be able to forget her? The one thing he knew was that he better not ever fall in love with her, because they had no future and he would be miserable.

He could never ever be happy married to her. He had old-fashioned ideas and he believed in them. In the first place, he didn't want to return to Thane's ranch and have an affair with Thane's widow. That was breaking a deep, important trust that his best friend had in him. She was so off limits for him. In addition, he didn't want to marry her and work for her and have her support him. That was ingrained in him by his dad since he was a kid. And after his dad died, by his oldest brother—the man earns the money and has the money. He does not take money from women. He would never be a billionaire, not in his wildest dreams, and he couldn't cope with that.

He entered the empty guesthouse and stood in the center of the living room. He looked around, not knowing what to do next. His thoughts were on Vivian. How was he going to be able to go out with her again next Friday night? It couldn't take many times to convince Clint that she was interested in another man. But Mike couldn't take many more nights like this one. He wanted to keep his promise, do what he should regarding Thane's wife and his ranch, but temptation was monumental with Vivian.

He couldn't take kissing her again.

Vivian walked into the mansion without seeing her surroundings. Her lips still tingled and her breath still trembled. She'd had a wonderful time tonight. Mike was fun when he wasn't being stodgy. She smiled when she remembered telling him he was stuffy. She had seen the surprised look on his face and then the determined look. The alpha male had risen to the bait.

She'd wanted Mike to kiss her. Even now, the realization struck her like a lightning bolt as it had earlier tonight when they were dancing. Ever since Thane's death, she'd been closed off, isolated both physically here on the ranch and emotionally. But tonight she had felt different. Ready to have fun, to live. For six months, people had been telling her that Thane would want her to go on with her life. Tonight, for the first time, she understood them. She was certain her one true love would want her to live, just as she was certain that if it was the other way around, she would want Thane to go on.

Had Thane sent Mike to marry her?

The thought pulled her up short, but she laughed. That hardheaded…

She laughed. That hardheaded, old-fashioned man wouldn't marry her even if he was wildly in love with her. She knew he felt honor bound to come home and take care of Thane's ranch, but to keep his distance from her. And right now he wasn't in love and neither was she.

She looked around the room and her eyes lit on Thane's picture on the mantel. She picked up the silver frame. "I love you," she whispered to him, knowing he was never coming back to her. She sat down, holding the picture against her heart with one hand while the other hand wiped the tears that slid down her face. "Thane, I miss you," she said softly as she sobbed. It hurt and she wondered if she would cry the rest of her life.

After a time, she dried her tears, trying to focus on the present. For a little while tonight, she had had fun with Mike. He was exciting and his kisses made her hot, dizzy with longing. It had been exhilarating to flirt and dance and kiss him. Until she had looked up and seen Clint at the door to the patio. He'd watched Mike with such an enraged, hateful expression that in that moment she had been frightened. But Mike hadn't been frightened at all and that had reassured her.

Mike seemed so certain, so calm about Clint that it had eased her fears and actually made her forget all about her insidious neighbor.

The delightful evening had been too brief. Mike had driven away her loneliness and grief for a little while and made her laugh and enjoy life again. Her lips still tingled and she wondered whether she would sleep at all tonight. Excitement still filled her and she felt as if she had swallowed bubbles that were dancing inside her. She could have danced until they closed the place, and next Friday, she intended to make a full evening of it.

She knew she should be careful, because she didn't want to fall in love with Mike. She could tease him into kissing her, but he wasn't the man for her to fall in love with, because she had been through one giant heartache when she lost the love of her life. Mike had given her only three months and then he would possibly move on. She didn't want another heartbreak. She hurt enough now. Besides, he was an outdated alpha male through and through who would hold to his backward ideas about women and life. He would never be able to get past her income unless he won billions in the lottery that would put him on the same financial level with her inheritance.

Reality took some shine off her excitement and she sighed. She shouldn't want to go out with him as much as she did. Right now, she was too vulnerable. Mike Moretti would never be the man for her to fall in love with. He would be a heartbreaker.

She sighed and tried to stop thinking about Mike. When she couldn't sleep, she went to her studio and began to paint. The painting needed to be finished tomorrow to be shipped to Austin for a gallery showing on Thursday.

Then the day after that she would go out with Mike again. Would that be the last time or would they have to keep going out for several more weekends? Maybe it was the novelty of being social again that was so great after such a long time without having an evening out with someone exciting. She told herself the novelty might wear off.

"Right," she said out loud.

She picked up the brush and gave herself some much-needed advice as she applied the first stroke of paint.

"Forget him, Vivian." If she didn't, he could walk away in three months and take her heart with him. She didn't want to deal with another big heartbreak.

If it was only that easy to do.

On Thursday afternoon, Mike was driving across the ranch in his pickup to meet Slade who was moving some cattle from one pasture to another when his phone buzzed. Seeing the call was from Vivian who was in Austin for her showing, so he stopped and answered.

"Hi. How's the gallery show going?" he asked, curious why she had time to call.

"Mike, Clint has been in. He knew I was having a showing here and he wanted me to go to dinner with him. Of course, I'm not going."

Her pronouncement had his stomach in angry knots. The guy just didn't give up.

Vivian went on. "Ben drove me this morning, but I'm trying to get in touch with Henry. I'd like him to come to Austin and ride back with us. Clint made me nervous today. He was very persistent and I think he'll be back. Can you find Henry? Get him to drive here and get one of the guys to ride with him and drive his car back. I'd feel better if Henry rode back with us."

He could hear the tension in her voice. "Sure thing. Don't worry and get Ben to hang out with you in the gallery."

"He is. I know this is silly because Clint is simply a pest, but I don't like having him around me."

"Don't let him worry you. He's a creep, but he's harmless, only a nuisance. Ben's there. We'll get rid of Clint. Enjoy your show. And think about going out with me Friday night. You might even get a chance to goad me into kissing you again."

She laughed. "Okay, I feel better now."

"Good. You'll be home before you know it."

"Thanks, Mike."

As soon as the call ended, Mike called Slade instead of Henry. As it rang, he got into his pickup and when he ended the call, he headed back to the guesthouse.

Vivian stood with a customer who had purchased a painting, which was being packaged and wrapped for him to take home.

"I hope you enjoy your painting. Thank you," Vivian said. "I enjoyed meeting you and talking to you."

The man nodded. "My wife is going to like this picture, I'm sure."

"Have a fun time tonight at her birthday party."

"I think the painting will be the highlight of the evening."

She smiled as Ben picked up the painting to carry it to the car for the customer. As he left, she looked outside the gallery window and her heart skipped. Was it really Mike standing outside talking to the man who had just purchased her painting? Her gaze raced over his matching white hat and shirt, brown jacket, a bolo tie, jeans and boots. It was every inch Mike and then he turned toward the door.

Suddenly self-conscious, she glanced at a mirror that hung across the room and straightened her deep blue suit jacket. She shook her hair away from her face and smiled as Mike came through the door. There was no way to ignore the rush she felt when she looked into his green eyes.

He looked so handsome, strong and solid that the sight of him made her want to hug him. "How'd you get here so quickly? I talked to you only a little more than an hour ago."

"I had Jason fly me here. Henry's parking the rental car. He can ride back with Ben. You and I will fly back to the ranch."

"I feel ridiculous, but Clint bothered me. He wanted me to go to dinner tonight and stay over in Austin. I've never gone out with him once, so why would he think I'd go to dinner and stay over?"

"Don't ask me how Clint Woodson's mind works."

Henry came through the door. "Hi, Vivian, Ben."

"Thanks for coming, Henry," she said.

"Sure. Glad to. That's my job. How's it going?" he said, turning to Ben.

The cowboy shrugged. "Okay. Woodson's been in once, but I'm betting that he'll be back."

Vivian looked at Mike. "It's been quiet and peaceful other than Clint and he really didn't do anything to disturb anyone except me. Clint came in when Ben went to lunch. The morning was busy and pleasant and the gallery people were here along with some friends."

She turned and called out to the gallery owner. "Marta, come meet some people from our ranch." The tall brunette held her hand out to Mike as Vivian introduced him and then Henry.

She brought over three more women connected with the gallery, and then finally she and Mike were alone again.

"I'll look around, and Henry and me will hang

out for the rest of the afternoon," he told her. "What about the paintings? Do they go home later?"

"Not now. The gallery wants to show them, so they'll be here for a couple of months."

She watched Mike walk around the room. He took his hat off and disappeared in the direction of the offices and reappeared shortly without it. While he was gone, Marta appeared to ask about a painting and Vivian had a chance to give her a brief explanation of why Mike and Henry had appeared, telling Marta Clint was harmless, but too insistent on wanting her to go out with him.

She was busy with customers and art lovers until after four o'clock when there was finally a lull. But instead of relaxing, she tensed up when she looked out the window. She walked over to Mike where he sat in a chair quietly talking to Ben and Henry. "I just saw Clint drive up and park out front."

Mike stood. "Henry, I think you two can hang where you are. At least for right now." Mike put his arm around Vivian's waist. They both turned as the bell over the door sounded.

The minute Mike touched her, Vivian stopped thinking about anyone else. She was keenly aware of his arm lightly around her as he stood close, holding her against his side.

"Mr. Woodson," Mike said, nodding.

Clint glanced around at the men, nodding and giving a cursory hello. "I see you brought help along," he said, smiling at her. "Have you had a good showing? I sent some people over."

"Yes, I have. I've been busy all day."

"Hello, again, Mr. Woodson. Do you want to see some more paintings?" Marta asked, approaching him.

"Sure. I might buy one this time." He walked off with Marta while she talked about the paintings.

"Thanks for being here," Vivian said quietly to Mike. "I don't even want him to own one of my paintings, but I can't do anything about that. Except hope he'll leave when he finishes the transaction."

"Come on. Let's go into Marta's office and wait until he's gone," Mike replied. "Henry, Ben, we'll be in the back." The men nodded and Mike put his arm around her shoulders to walk down the hall. Clint glanced at them as they passed the room where he stood listening to Marta tell him about a painting.

They stepped into Marta's office and Mike closed the door, removing his arm from Vivian's shoulders. Instantly, she felt the loss.

"Mike, I've been thinking about it. Clint pops up whenever I leave the ranch. Someone must be telling him where I'll be. It gives me the creeps for him to be around when I leave town." She felt a shudder dance over her spine. "I've also been thinking about this. Maybe you should move into the main house at the ranch. I already have Henry and Millie and Francie living in my house. There are big suites and all kinds of entrances and exits. You wouldn't have to see me and you could come and go as you please where you wouldn't see anyone else. If you moved into my house, word would get around and—"

He smiled. "Stop. That house is bigger than some hotels I've stayed in. Yes, I'll move in. If that doesn't get rid of Clint, I don't know what will. You know, he's probably paying someone who works for you to tell him where you are."

"That's annoying if it's my employee."

"He's probably paying a lot and he probably makes it sound harmless. I think he is harmless, just a creep, an annoying bully. He wants you and he wants your ranch but we'll get rid of him," he said.

"You're always so confident."

"Only when I know I'm right," he said, and she smiled.

"You sure you're okay with moving in?"

He nodded. " I'll stay for a few weeks. Word will get back to Clint and that should do it. Besides, that and seeing us today with my arm around you and the other night kissing out on the terrace, he'll get the message. He can't be that dense."

"I feel sure we'll see him this Friday night. We're going to an old downtown Dallas club. We belong and so does Clint. I can't imagine that all this won't run him off soon."

"I agree." Mike gave her a long look that made her breath catch and then he crossed the room to her. The closer he came, the faster her heart beat. He didn't pause, but wrapped his arms around her. She noticed his aftershave, an enticing woodsy scent. His green eyes had tiny gold flecks near the center, his slight stubble that showed on his jaw added to his already tough look, and his black tousled hair curled on his forehead.

"Maybe we should give him something to think about," Mike said. He wrapped his arms around her, looked at her as if to see if she agreed and then he kissed her.

Four

The minute his lips met hers, she forgot everything else. Her world became Mike, his arms, his body, his mouth and what they were doing to her. Her heart pounded and she clung to him. He wound one hand in her hair as he held her tightly. Desire heated her and for a moment she forgot where she was or why she was there. He was solid, exciting, sexy and he made her feel alive again.

When he released her, she felt dazed as she looked into green eyes that had darkened with obvious desire. He took out a handkerchief to wipe her lip gloss off his face and then touched it to the corner of her mouth, wiping gently. He unbuttoned the top button of her white silk blouse. "That adds to the effect."

"That one button is barely noticeable, but it's enough," she added hastily.

"Clint will notice. I'll see what's going on. Come join us when you want."

"We look like we've kissed."

The corner of his mouth lifted in a crooked smile. "I think we did. I must not have made an impression."

"You know you did," she said softly. "You rocked my world." She crossed the room to a mirror to look at herself.

"I thought you wanted to give Clint the impression that you and I are a couple."

"I do and I will if he sees me now." She ran her fingers through her hair and shook her head. "But we'll probably shock Henry and Ben."

"I imagine they'll both know exactly what we're trying to do. They know you're trying to run him off."

She sighed. "You're right." She joined him and he held the door, stepping out behind her and then closing it. He held her arm as they walked down the hall together.

Clint stood near the door talking to Marta. He glanced at Vivian and his eyes narrowed slightly as he looked from her to Mike and back again. "I bought one of your paintings, Vivian. I'll think of you when I look at it," he said. "Marta is having it sent to my house in Dallas."

"Thank you, Clint," she said quietly while Mike stood at her side. He was looking at a small pocket reminder book he carried and he made a note in it. She glanced back at Clint whose gaze raked insolently over her.

"Well, I'll leave you to your art show," he said. He turned and left, causing the little bell over the door to ring as the door opened then shut.

"He won't be back today," Mike said, "so I'll join the guys. Anything you want, let me know."

"Anything I want?" she asked softly in a sultry tone.

He'd been about to turn away, but he turned back to her and stepped close again. "Vivian, you're flirting and you're going to get yourself in trouble if you aren't careful," he said almost in a whisper.

"Oh, I'll be careful, Mike, but you asked me."

He shook his head and walked away while she grinned.

The bell rang and Marta stepped to the door. Three women entered and wanted to meet Vivian and see her paintings. Vivian was busy for the next two hours and then it was time to close the gallery.

It took another hour to get everything recorded, divided up and put away. Finally, she turned to look at Mike. "Are we flying home now?"

"Yes, you and I. Henry will ride back with Ben so we're set. I called a few minutes ago and told Jason to get the plane ready." He turned to face Marta who was straightening a picture on the wall. "Marta, it was nice to meet you. Thank you for what you did today."

He moved closer to Vivian. "Just let us know

when you're ready and Ben will drop us off at the airport."

"I'm ready." She turned to Marta to thank her again for the showing. They talked briefly about the paintings and then left. Outside, Vivian turned to Henry. "Thanks, Henry, for flying with Mike."

"Sure. Ben will drop you two off at the plane and then we'll head back to the ranch."

"Thank you," she repeated.

"Thanks, guys," Mike said. At the small private airport, Ben drove past three hangars and stopped near the waiting Tumbling T plane. In minutes they were onboard, seated with their seat belts fastened. She watched out the window while the limo turned in a circle and left.

"From a work standpoint, this was a fun, successful day. I saw friends, showed my art, made new friends and sold some of my paintings, which is nice. Then again, there was Clint." She turned to Mike and looked him in the eyes. "Thank you, Mike, for coming to my rescue. Clint is a pest, but I feel sure he'll be gone soon."

"I haven't run him off yet."

Jason, their pilot, announced they had been cleared for takeoff and she looked out the window for a moment as the plane gained speed and then lifted and was airborne.

"Mike, I have another favor to ask you," she said, voicing what she had been thinking about all morning. She took a deep breath, hoping her question wouldn't send him running. "Mike, when we talked about you moving into my house…well, there's a lot of room and you can live where you never have to see—"

He cut her off. "I told you I don't mind. It won't be permanent and if it helps get rid of Clint, it's all worth it. If someone from the ranch is keeping him posted on where you are and what you're doing, then he's sure to get the report that I'm in the house."

"But not anywhere near me." She paused a moment, gathering her courage to voice her request. "Would you consider moving into the big suite at the end of the hall from mine? If you're there, on the same floor and not too far away, no one will know how much we go back-and-forth to each other's suites."

He didn't hesitate. "I think that would be best. I'll even come to your suite at night if you think we need to do that," he said, and she saw the sparkle in his eyes and knew he was teasing.

"Seriously, Mike, you were inconvenienced today and you'll get paid extra for it. I'll do the same for Henry. Ben gets paid to do this, but he'll get extra for this trip."

Mike looked at her a moment before he finally nodded. "Okay, thanks," he said and she felt as if he thanked her simply out of courtesy and he really didn't want her to pay him extra at all.

He was an old-fashioned guy, she thought, wondering why she had such an intense physical reaction to him when she couldn't understand his outdated ideas. "You don't like taking money from me, do you? If Thane was here with you and he made that offer, you'd say thanks and like it and never give it another thought."

"You might be right. Vivian, I grew up with a dad who died when I was thirteen. There were four kids in our family and my mom was a high school drop-out. My oldest brother was like a dad to me. My two older brothers went to college, got jobs and helped put me through college. I went with their help and with scholarships and the money I made working my own jobs. And winning in rodeos. Mostly bull riding and calf roping. I graduated, got a job on a ranch and helped put my youngest brother through school. Now all of us help take care of Mom. It hasn't been easy. I got my ideas from my dad and my oldest brother after my dad wasn't around. And for some reason, they probably are old-fashioned. But, Vivian, wherever my ideas come from, surely you can see you're way out of my league," he said quietly.

"It shouldn't be such an issue. Life's more important than money."

"Well, it's a little different when you don't have any."

With his words, she felt a wall rising up between them and suspected he would never change his views. "You were friends with Thane and you didn't seem to care what he had."

"That's entirely different."

She laughed. "To someone in the last century."

He gave her a crooked smile that made her tingle.

Even arguing with him was fun and she couldn't understand her own response to him.

Mike leaned closer. "Sweetie, Clint will get out of your life. I'll go back to living in the guesthouse house and who knows, maybe I'll move on myself, someday. I'll be out of your way and you won't have to put up with me and my old-fashioned ways."

"Well, maybe," she said, gazing into his green eyes. "But right now, you like to kiss me and when you do, you forget about all those rules you have about what a man does and what a woman does."

She was slightly exasperated with him and his antiquated views of her wealth. And she couldn't stop thinking about his kiss in Marta's office. A kiss that made her want more. He had to have felt something because he'd looked as startled and as filled with desire as she'd felt.

"You, darlin', stir up trouble easier than a gnat finding fruit," he said.

"My kisses are trouble? Imagine that. I thought they were quite harmless," she said, teasing him and having fun in the process, wondering if she could goad him into another sexy kiss.

"See, you know you're doing it right now. For you, my kiss may be as harmless as watching the clouds roll by, but when I kiss you, it's as dangerous to me as jumping into a fire and you know it. And, Vivian, you're pushing right now." He unbuckled his seat belt and turned to slip an arm behind her as he leaned over.

She started to reply, but when his mouth covered

hers, whatever she had been about to say was gone forever. Her heart raced as he kissed her passionately, a demanding kiss that made her forget their silly conversation and her teasing. His lips started a fire low inside her. She wanted the seat belt out of the way. She wanted her arms around him and his around her and she wanted every inch of him pressed against her. Every barrier between them gone.

His kiss was pure seduction. Her breasts tingled, her body ached for his hands, his mouth, all of him. Common sense, resistance, wisdom burned away in the first few seconds. All she knew was she wanted him to keep touching her and kissing her and to never stop. Dimly she was aware of the release of her seat belt and his hand drifting in circles over her breast. She moaned as she held him tightly, running her fingers over him, down over a bicep as hard as a rock.

She felt his fingers unbuttoning her blouse before releasing the catch on her bra and then cool air on her bare skin and then his tongue, hot, wet, trailing down over her bare breasts. "Mike," she whispered and pushed lightly against him.

Instantly, there was space between them as he rose slightly and she looked up at him. Desire, making his eyes darker, was so obvious that she trembled. "We don't have any privacy and we're about to go where each one of us knows we shouldn't."

"Vivian, you know what to do to get me going. Don't do it unless you want to deal with me and with the results."

She bit back a teasing reply because he looked

pushed over a limit and she wasn't ready to go any further, and they didn't have privacy on the plane anyway.

"Okay, Mike," she said, feeling subdued even as her heart still raced and her body quivered with desire. She wanted him. She wanted his arms around her, his mouth on hers again, his tongue and fingers making her come to life and feel loved and desired once again. She had been so alone, so lonesome and now Mike was driving all that away, most of the time in fun, but not now. Now it was a blaze of hot, passionate kisses and caresses that were headed straight for a fantastic seduction.

She closed her eyes for a moment, trying to get control, to get the sexy thoughts out of her mind, to return to a normal afternoon with two employees. Knowing that wasn't going to happen, she opened her eyes to find Mike intently watching her. There were moments when his intent looks seemed to go right through her and she felt as if he could discern every thought she had.

She straightened her clothes and glanced toward the cockpit, thankful for the panel that kept her seat from Jason's view. He might see Mike, but he was back in his seat, his seat belt on.

She cast a look his way and saw he was still aroused. She too tingled all over, but wisdom had finally returned and she was hanging on to it like a lifeline in a crisis. Only that wisdom could tell her what she should do.

She had looked forward to this showing at the

Austin gallery, and it had been successful, but the only part of the day she would remember was Mike. Long after she had forgotten the rest of the day and the people in it, she'd recall him and his kisses.

Once again, a familiar thought ran through her mind. Had Thane sent Mike because he knew Mike would run the ranch the way Thane wanted it ran?

Or had he sent Mike because he knew Mike would fill a lonely void in her life?

It would be just like Thane. When he was alive, all he'd wanted to do was take care of her. He had loved the fact that they were together out on the ranch, far from her father. He'd even urged Vivian to not move right away if something were to happen to him. He'd told her to take her time, let things settle and then decide. Several times he had reminded her that she couldn't go back once she moved away. Was her wonderful late husband trying to take care of her from beyond the grave?

Mike interrupted her thoughts. "Are you okay? You're quiet."

"Thanks to you. I'm on fire and you know it."

He took her hand lightly, casually holding it. "Well, we both got ourselves into a twist then. To calm things down, let's talk about what you want to do when we get in. We can have Jason change the flight plan and land in Dallas. We can go to dinner there and drive back to the ranch. Or we can fly back to the ranch," he said and released her hand.

"The ranch is fine." She turned to look out the window and settle herself. After a few minutes she thought she'd put it all in perspective. "Mike, it's been a long time since Thane was home. I stay on the ranch and paint, so I don't see a lot of friends. Maybe I've just gotten carried away with you around."

"I hope so. It's fun, Vivian, but we're both being reckless. I've been in a war zone and you've been through a loss and living isolated in a lot of ways. Maybe—" He stopped himself. "Forget it. I take things too seriously sometimes."

"Ah, good," she said, feeling better and smiling. "You've got your sense back."

"Sort of," he said. "Though if I had any sense, I'd sit across the aisle from you."

She put her chin in her hand, her elbow on the armrest and looked closely at him. "I do that to you?"

"See, dammit! You and I need to get out and circulate more. We can't keep from flirting and teasing each other when we both know where it will lead and neither one of us wants that."

"Oh, speak for yourself, cowboy," she said, laughing and sitting back, getting out a magazine from her tote bag. "I'll sit and read and leave you in peace and quiet. Hey, look at this," she said, pointing to the shout line on the bottom right of the cover.

He twisted slightly to read aloud: "'How to Keep the Man in Your Life Happy.'" He looked up at her. "Vivian—"

She smiled at him, unable to resist teasing him. "I'd say right now you're the man in my life. Don't you think? Well, I know exactly what will keep you happy. Leave you alone like an old bear in its den."

"Correct. You do that. You're finally getting on the right track."

"Watch out, Mike. You'll hurt my feelings."

"No, I won't, and we won't argue that point. I'll nap."

She laughed. "Of course, you will. I'm sure you feel so sleepy now." He gave her a look of exasperation that made her be quiet. He turned his back to her and placed his head against the seat. She knew he wasn't napping, but he was tuning her out and she suspected she needed to leave well enough alone— they'd had a passionate moment that still resounded for both of them.

She looked at the back of his head, his neat haircut that was probably due to the military influence. He was fun to tease, irresistible and sexy and exciting. And dangerous to her well-being. She knew he would never fall in love with her and if she did fall in love with him, she would have nothing but heartbreak. He would never get past her income, her inheritance and her position as his boss. How had he gotten that way? Was it from the tough times he'd had growing up when they were so short of money? Was she so accustomed to her wealthy dad that she didn't give her status and bank account a thought?

All she knew was that she should keep her distance from Mike, guard her heart and use more sense around him. But he was too appealing, too sexy and she had been too lonely after Thane's death. From the very first moment she'd met him, when they'd shaken hands, there had been a sizzling reaction that she knew he felt, too. How could she resist that?

With a sigh she turned away, looking down at the magazine cover and smiling over showing it to him. "How to Keep the Man in Your Life Happy." Well, in reality, the only man who really wanted to be in her life was a pest she was trying to get rid of. The man seated next to her was trying to ignore her and he sure wasn't in her life except to be in her employ. She did have a date with him, though, for Friday night. Granted, it was at her own request, but it was a date nonetheless. When they were out together, he couldn't resist flirting any more than she could. And he could dance and was fun in spite of trying not to be, the way he was right now. She smiled and almost reached out to run her hand over his, but she didn't.

He had come through for her this afternoon, taking her call and acting on it immediately. She was certain if there had been any way to save Thane, Mike would have found it. He kept a cool head in a crisis. Mike, Henry, Ben, Jason, Slade—Thane had done well in the men he had hired. The only one that wasn't a responsible, stand-up guy was Leon, but Thane couldn't have known that because he was all Thane had hoped when Thane had been home. Come to think of it, Leon must have gone back to that type of guy now. She hadn't heard a word about him from Mike and she hadn't seen Leon anywhere near her. Maybe Mike's presence was an influence on the horse trainer. Now she could only hope he had the same influence on Clint Woodson.

* * *

When they landed at the ranch, Mike's pickup was parked near the hangar. He held the pickup door for her and closed it, going around to get in the driver's seat.

Once they were on the road, Vivian resumed the discussion of his move. "If you can, why don't you move into the house next Saturday? I'm sure you can get some guys to help if you need it."

"All I have to move is my clothes. I'm assuming the suite in the main house is fully furnished like the guesthouse?"

"Yes, it is."

"Then I won't need help moving."

"You should still make sure some of the guys know what you're doing. After all, I want word to get back to Clint."

"It'll get back to him and the guys will know. You can't dig up dandelions around here without everyone knowing it."

She brought up the subject of the horse trainer that she'd thought about on the plane. "Mike, what about Leon? You've never mentioned him."

"No need to. He hasn't been up to the house, has he?"

"Not at all."

"He won't come around. Word is out that I was close with Thane. Slade likes me and word is also out that you and I are friends. That's enough for a man like Leon. He doesn't have the money or the clout that Clint does, so he isn't going to cause trouble. You've seen the last of him unless you hunt him down."

"That's good to hear."

They were both quiet until Mike stopped the pickup at the mansion and walked her up to the porch. At the door, Vivian turned to him. "So I'll see you Friday night. I thought we could stay at my penthouse condo in downtown Dallas. That way, Ben can go do what he wants Friday night after he drops us off. My family owns three condos near mine and near Dad's office. Ben and his wife stay in one when they're in Dallas. Henry and Millie stay in the other, so they'll be close at hand. And, my old-fashioned friend, my penthouse condo is big. You can have your own suite and I wouldn't dream of trying to seduce you," she said in a sultry voice, unable to resist flirting even though she didn't want to fall in love with him She reminded herself he would go out of her life as suddenly as he came into it.

"Vivian, you're pulling my chain again," he replied in a husky voice.

She smiled sweetly because she saw the sparkle in his eyes. "Well, the last time I did that I got a big kiss. What will happen this time?"

He stepped close and put his hands on either side of her face, turning her head so she had to look up at him. "I think you like to kiss and you want to kiss. And, darlin', I will oblige," he said, and his mouth covered hers.

A wave of desire poured over her, hot, tingling, steamy need that made her want him to hold her the rest of the night and kiss her and let her hold and kiss him. Her heart pounded and she slipped her arms around his narrow waist, holding him tightly, feeling his hard body against her, his muscles and long legs.

He broke the kiss and looked down into her eyes. In their green depths she saw blatant longing. "Mike," she whispered, all teasing forgotten.

He accepted the unspoken invitation in her word and his mouth claimed hers again. He kissed her long and passionately, making her heart drum, making her forget all the reasons she didn't want to get too close to him.

When he released her, he looked at her intently. "I need to get out of here for both our sakes. Good night, Vivian." He brushed a kiss on her cheek and hurried to his pickup, driving away without looking back.

She stood a moment, watching him drive into the darkness. His kisses had melted her and at the same time stirred a sweeping need for hours of loving in a strong man's arms. She missed her husband, missed so much about him. But there was something about Mike that drew her to him. Something she was having a hard time denying. Till she remembered… Mike was too ingrained in his old-fashioned beliefs and he'd never get past her inheritance. Ironic, she thought, because there were men out there who would want the inheritance more than they would want her.

Mike had been good to come today when she needed someone. He came and brought Henry and he would move into her house for a brief time. She should leave him alone, not get too close. He wasn't going to stay. Slade had warned her and he should know. Mike could break her heart if she fell in love with him, and she was still living with heartache over losing the only man she'd ever loved.

She missed Thane every day. He had been hell-bent on enlisting, serving his country, doing his patriotic duty. His grandfather fought in Korea. His dad fought in Vietnam. Because of family tradition, Thane had felt he owed his country some service. If only she could have gotten pregnant, she might have been able to hold him at home; but their attempts hadn't been successful before he'd left. The doctor had assured her she'd be able to conceive if she just relaxed, but that had been easier said than done when Thane was making plans to join the Rangers.

Now she was alone and vulnerable because of her loss. Too vulnerable. She needed to take care with Mike.

She had no illusions. Mike was a tough ex-ranger. He knew self-discipline and control and he didn't want to love an heiress, a woman who had more money and power than he did, and he would stick by that conviction with that iron control he had. When his promise to Thane was up, he would be gone. She didn't have a single doubt about that. Neither did Slade. She sighed. "You sent home a reliable guy, Thane. But I wish you'd sent one who could bend a little and be more like you."

She thought about Mike's kiss today. He could set her on fire with longing and need.

Tomorrow night she was going out with him. Even if he didn't like taking her out, he was fun and she'd miss that when he stopped. When Clint got out of her life, Mike would, too. Until then, she'd have a blast at the club. She had shed buckets of tears over her lost love and over being alone. Friday night, she planned to have a good time and Mike would help her do just that.

Friday night, Mike wore a charcoal suit with matching boots, his black Stetson and a black-and-gray striped tie. They were going to an old established club in downtown Dallas, a club that once had been men only. Then they would go back to Vivian's penthouse condo. He sighed and warned himself one more time to use some common sense and to avoid letting her get to him, teasing him into losing control again. It was difficult to resist her taunts. He knew she was being playful, but that made her all the more irresistible. That and knowing what it was like to kiss her.

He could kiss her all night long and it wouldn't be enough. She was incredibly sexy and her body had luscious curves. She was soft, but she had her feisty moments when he lost it and wanted to grab and kiss her.

He wanted to run Clint off and be able to stay away from Vivian before she snagged his heart, then it would hurt like hell to leave her.

In the meantime, he couldn't wait to go out with her.

Then next week he'd be moving into her mansion.

He strode up the walk, the waiting limo behind him, and looked up at the massive house. He couldn't even imagine the cost of building such a home out on this mesquite-covered prairie.

When he entered the front door, Henry held the door.

"I thought you're off on Friday night."

"I am. I leave when you two do. Millie and I are going into Dallas for the weekend. So I'll see you Monday morning unless you have an emergency. You have my number."

"We better not have an emergency. Did she tell you I'm moving into this place next week?"

"Yes, she did. Good idea. That ought to finish Clint being in her life. And it won't be any hardship to have another person live here. You could drop a hotel inside this house and still have room. I think Thane thought they would fill it with kids, friends and relatives, but life doesn't work out the exact way you plan most of the time." He shrugged. "Have a good time tonight. Millie and I've been out with her a few times, but she's been shut up alone here for too long. She'll probably wear you down."

"Yeah, well, I'm ready to party myself. There wasn't much partying where I was last year."

Henry nodded, and Mike knew the ex-marine could relate firsthand to what he was talking about. "I'll see you. And next week I can help you move."

"Sure. Have a good time, Henry. Hopefully, there won't be a peep out of us."

As he watched Henry walk down the hall, a voice from behind startled him.

"Have you been waiting long?"

He turned to see Vivian coming down the sweeping spiral staircase. She wore a pale blue dress of some soft fabric that swirled around her knees with each step she took. Thane's diamond pendant glittered in the light. Mike's heart thudded and beat twice as fast. Vivian looked like a dream. Her blond hair fell on her shoulders, turning up slightly. The sleeveless dress emphasized her tiny waist and the high-heeled sandals highlighted her long shapely legs. He wanted to take her into his arms and kiss her while he scooped her up and found the closest bedroom.

That wasn't going to happen. He needed to constantly remember Thane sent him to take care of Vivian. She was so off-limits to him. He smiled and said hello and told her Ben was outside with the limo.

She gave him a dazzling smile. "I'm ready for some excitement."

He took her arm and they left, going to the limo, and soon they were on their way to Dallas. He sat close to her and she placed her hand lightly on his knee. He wondered how aware she was of touching him. It was a casual touch on her part, but the result wasn't casual to him. He had an instant reaction to her hand on his leg. He didn't want to make an issue of it, so he kept quiet and tried to talk about something that would take his mind off his arm around her or how close she sat, lightly pressed against him, her hand on his leg.

He tried, but he couldn't stop his awareness of her. Or the trepidation that had been building in him all day. Was he being driven in a long white limo to a destination that would change his life? He didn't think so, but he also didn't want to get hurt badly. Falling in love with Vivian could be disastrous. He was holding the hand of Thane's wife and he couldn't get past that.

The club was on the top floor of one of the tallest buildings in Dallas. Through the floor-to-ceiling windows they could look out on the glittering lights of the city below. The band was good and the crowd already partying.

They ordered drinks and sat at a table for two. When the drinks came, he raised his eyes, looking over the rim of his glass into her big blue eyes. "Here's to you, Vivian. May you get what you want in life to make up for what you lost in the past."

"I'll drink to that," she said, holding up her glass and touching it lightly to his crystal goblet. She watched him as she sipped and he wanted to skip dinner, skip dancing and go to that penthouse condo of hers and make love to her all night long. But if he didn't want his life in a tangled snarl, he shouldn't do any such thing. He should stay right here, party, enjoy looking at her, flirt with her a little, relish in her company and dance with her, but avoid with all his being getting any more entangled with this woman.

His gaze shifted to her full red lips and he drew a deep breath, remembering how those lips felt beneath his. He looked up to meet her wide-eyed gaze that held desire, a come-hither look that set him on fire.

"Let's dance, Mike," she whispered. "I need to move around. I've looked forward to this all day long." In minutes they were on the dance floor, dancing to a lively number, and he watched her as she moved around him with abandon. The more he was with her the more he wanted her in his bed. Get through tonight, he told himself. One day at a time and soon he would be away from her.

After dinner he shed his jacket and got down to dancing in earnest, ending two fast songs with one slow ballad, finally taking her into his arms to hold her close. She smelled wonderful and was as soft as he had remembered.

Holding her, he couldn't help but anticipate the rest of the night at her penthouse. They'd be alone, just the two of them, and he envisioned doing all the things to her that had kept him up at night. But he didn't dare. He shouldn't even think about it. It would be smarter to stay here at the club until it closed, to be with people and avoid getting in a situation in the condo where he would kiss away his determination to not complicate his life.

Vivian looked as if she was having the time of her life and he felt a clutch in his heart as he thought about Thane, remembering those last moments of holding his friend and trying to stop his blood from flowing away. She and Thane had loved each other and she'd had a lot of lonesome months since his death. She was isolated on the ranch. She had Henry and Millie and Francie to talk to, but Henry was out doing things and Millie had her work, and Mike doubted if she hung out in the kitchen with Francie very much. He was surprised she had remained on the ranch this long, except that it was one last tie to Thane that hadn't been broken.

"I think it's time to move on," she finally said about the same time the band stopped playing. He nodded and walked back to the table with her to get her purse. Her condo was close and it was a nice night so they walked. As he left the club, he wondered if he was walking straight into heartbreak.

Five

Noticing her perfume again as he walked beside her, Mike wanted her in his arms and he was having a silent argument with himself. It would be best to tell her good-night and go to his room and lock himself in there. But that wasn't what he wanted to do at all.

He tried to think of all the reasons not to get intertwined with her. First of all, she was Thane's wife. Even though Thane was no longer living, Mike felt there was some unspoken agreement that when Thane asked him to take the job of running the ranch, and he accepted, that he would not cause her heartbreak or any unhappiness. He also felt certain Thane didn't send him to the ranch to seduce her.

She was his boss. That would be bad business.

She was his friend's wife, his close friend who had hired him to help her and look out for her. Any time he touched her, he felt he was breaking an honored trust. She was the daughter of a billionaire. She had inherited Thane's millions, making her wealthy beyond his wildest dreams. She was accustomed to getting what she wanted, when she wanted it. He was not accustomed to having a woman like that in his life and he didn't like it and he didn't want to get emotionally wrapped up with her. And he damn well didn't want to fall in love with her. He could never buy her a ring or a necklace or any other thing that would be as beautiful as she could buy for herself. Not only the disparity between their incomes, but also when those three months were up , he was leaving. He wasn't going to live with this arrangement for years. He would have worked the three months he promised Thane.

"You're quiet, Mike."

His mind raced for a believable reason, because he certainly couldn't tell her the truth. "I was thinking about the ranch," he lied. "I think Slade will leave soon and he should. I'm urging him to go. I feel certain that it'll be sooner than he first said. He's decided I can take over and do his job and that frees him up to go."

"Do you feel ready to take it over?"

"Yes, I suppose I do. You take each problem as it comes."

"Then when he talks to you about it, do what you feel is best. As far as the ranch goes, you're

going to run it as if it's yours. That's what I need
and want. I don't know anything about it and running a ranch isn't my deal. Thane said I'd never have
to take charge." Her voice weakened on the last and
she looked away. He knew she hurt over Thane, and
Mike hurt because he couldn't do anything for her.

"Here we are," she said, stopping at a tall oil and
gas building. Lights were on in the lobby and an attendant sat at the desk. "There's the night watchman." Lights played over the front of the building,
so everything was well-lit and big flower boxes were
packed with multicolored blooming spring flowers.
She punched a button and Mike heard a beep and
clicks and then she opened a door.

He took Vivian's arm and they crossed an empty
lobby. The attendant at the desk said hello and called
Vivian by name. She answered and introduced Mike
to the night watchman.

After leaving the front desk, they stepped into the
elevator and it was a fast ride to the penthouse where
it opened directly into the condo.

As the doors closed behind Mike, she tossed her
purse on a table. He glanced around at an entryway that held a crystal chandelier, potted palms and
Queen Anne fruitwood chairs covered in a muted
design of red-and-blue damask. "Is this whole floor
yours?" he asked.

She nodded. "I told you there's plenty of room for
you to stay tonight."

Mike walked into the living area with floor-
to-ceiling windows that gave another panoramic view

of the sprawling city. It was even more breathtaking than the restaurant's view with all the twinkling lights. "This is spectacular." He turned to look at her and amended his thought. It was Vivian who was spectacular and took his breath away. The soft light spilled over her, highlighting her blond hair and creamy skin. He met her gaze and saw the desire in her eyes that he felt. It was hot, intense.

"Would you like a drink?"

"You know what I'd like," he said quietly. He couldn't look away. He was caught and held by her big blue eyes as he walked toward her. "I should get in that elevator and get the hell out of here. You and I don't belong together."

"Are you telling me you don't want to kiss me? I've seen the way you've looked at me all evening."

"I'm going to complicate my life and yours."

"You make way too big a deal out of it, but I'll tell you what, I'm not going to push you into kissing me." She raised her chin and turned to walk away. "I'll get us drinks—"

He stepped up and lightly placed his hand on her arm, turning her. She looked around with her eyes widening as surprise filled her expression. "Mike, don't kiss me if you don't—"

"You know damn good and well I want to kiss you with all my being," he said. His voice was gruff. "And you want me to kiss you. Come here, Vivian." He drew her to him, his mouth coming down on hers and coaxing her lips open as his tongue thrust inside.

Breathing heavily, he raised his head to look into

her eyes. "I want you. I want to kiss you the rest of the night, to hold you, to make love to you." He framed her face with his hands, his gaze searching hers. "You want me, too, don't you?"

"Yes," she whispered. "I want you to kiss me until I melt from loving. I want kisses that for tonight will stop heartaches and emptiness. Something to wipe all that out even briefly and something I can cling to in nights to come. Hot memories that don't leave me crying. I just want to feel alive with someone. I want to feel wanted, Mike, by a sexy, desirable man and I want to make you happy in return."

"You don't have to worry about that one, darlin'. Ah, Vivian if you'll take tonight—"

"Mike, I'll take whatever I can get," she said, brushing his mouth with hers. His heart felt as if it would pound out of his chest. He was aroused, aching with wanting her, wanting to kiss her senseless, to take her now, but he wasn't going to do any such thing. If they made love, he wanted to take a long time to give her all the pleasure and loving he could. He wanted to make her happy, leave her with the kind of memories she wanted. Do everything in his power to excite her and give her a night she could remember. He'd had his own cold, lonely nights, losses and hurts. Without even trying, he knew she would give him all the pleasure, memories, hot sex and excitement he craved.

He wrapped his arms around her and held her close to kiss her passionately. In minutes, he shifted, trailing kisses across her cheek, his tongue tracing the curve of her ear, his breath hot on her skin as he whispered, "I want to excite you as much as I possibly can, darlin'. I want to kiss and caress every beautiful inch of you and feel you moving and responding to my touch."

"Mike," she gasped, turning to kiss him.

He pulled her up tightly against him, holding her close, his tongue stroking hers while he slipped one hand down her back, unfastening her zipper and stroking her bare skin. He tangled his fingers in her hair and kissed her while she clung to him, moaning softly and kissing him in return. He wanted her with a need that felt like desperation. He wanted to spend the night with her in his arms. He'd tried to do the right thing. He'd tried to do the smart thing and walk away, but he couldn't and clearly she didn't want to, either.

She moaned softly, thrusting her hips against him, her hands playing over him as she opened the buttons of his shirt and tugged its shirttails out of his trousers. Desire swept over him and he leaned away slightly so he could pull the thin spaghetti straps of her blue dress off her shoulders. He slipped his arm around her and drew her close to kiss her again. As they kissed, he pushed her dress away and let it fall. It dropped in a puff and a whisper around her feet. When she stepped out of it, she left behind her shoes, as well.

The diamond pendant lay between the rise of her breasts. Mike touched it lightly, his fingers brushing her warm skin. "Do you always keep this on?"

"Yes, I do," she said.

He leaned back, placing his hands on her hips as he looked at her. She hadn't worn a bra beneath her dress and he cupped her bare breasts with his calloused hands. She wore only lacy bikini panties. "You're beautiful, darlin'. You take my breath away."

"Just kiss me, Mike," she whispered, clinging to him and leaning closer, her nipples brushing his chest. He cupped her breasts again, holding her. She was soft, filling his hands, so warm. He kissed first one breast and then the other, tracing each rosy peak with his tongue. "Ah, Vivian, you're beautiful and perfect. So soft, so gorgeous," he whispered.

She had her eyes closed, her head thrown back as she ran one hand through his hair and ran her other hand over his shoulder beneath his shirt. "I want this, Mike. I want you to kiss and hold me the rest of the night and drive away my hurt."

"Ah, Vivian. You shouldn't hurt and you shouldn't be lonely. You're too beautiful." He kissed her and she clung to him. He was aroused, his hard shaft between them, pressing into her. "Oh, baby, you should have a man's arms around you every night of your life. You were made to pleasure a man and take him to paradise." His gaze roamed over her. "I want you," he whispered hoarsely. "I want to kiss and touch you. We'll give each other tonight."

"I'm not protected. I'm not on the pill."

"I've got a condom." They looked into each other's eyes and he saw the desire he felt mirrored in her expression. He drew her to him to hold her naked body against his.

Wrapping her arms around his neck, Vivian stood on tiptoe to kiss him. "I want you, too," she said. "I want to kiss and touch you, to have it all for tonight."

The way she looked at him, the emotion he saw in her eyes, the need that reflected his own, all combined to take away the last of his control. In that moment, he wished he really could take away all her hurt. While he couldn't do that, he knew he could give her pleasure and he set about doing just that. He knew he was breaking all his rules and promises to himself. He wasn't avoiding trouble. Instead, he was running into heartache and regret with open arms. But he could no more stop and resist her now than he could quit his job and walk away. He wanted her more than he had ever desired any other woman. He might be tearing up his life for a long time to come, but he wanted Vivian this night. He wanted to hold and love her, give and take the excitement and pleasure of one night with her. This was the time and the opportunity and he wasn't going to back away from the most desirable woman he had ever known. He only hoped he could survive the consequences of tonight.

Vivian tingled from head-to-toe. Desire was hot, pulsing, an aching need, but she wanted this night to last, to make love for hours. There had been so many empty nights and now Mike was holding her, kissing her and making excitement race through her.

She pushed away his shirt, letting it fall while she unfastened his belt. She looked up and was caught in his hungry gaze. His slow perusal roamed over her body, and she trembled with eagerness, feeling as if he had drawn his fingers over her.

He took off his trousers and yanked away his socks and boots. He had on briefs that she peeled down to free him and then held and caressed his manhood that was hot and hard, ready for her. He held her hips lightly with his hands as she stroked him.

For a moment he let her take him in her mouth to run her tongue slowly over him, and then he pulled her up to trail kisses along her throat and down to her breasts, kissing first one and then the other, his tongue circling taut peaks, hot and wet, exciting her more.

Moaning softly with pleasure, she closed her eyes while he showered kisses on her and caressed her, feathery strokes that made her sigh softly.

Touching him, she explored his marvelous physique, discovering his body that was muscular and in peak shape. She tangled her fingers in the sprinkling of crisp, curly black hair across his chest. His chest was rock hard, all muscle, broad and warm as she trailed her hands over him.

With a low sound deep in his throat, he whispered in her ear. "I want you, Vivian. I want to make love to you all the rest of this night."

"That's what I want, too. To kiss and touch and

discover each other. I want to excite you and pleasure you every way you want."

"Ah, darlin'," he said, showering kisses on her breasts as he cupped them in his big hands. "You excite me just by letting me look at you. You'll never know how much I want you, more than you can possibly imagine. I've dreamed about you, fantasized about you, longed for you. I don't want to let you go until this night is over and the sun is high in the sky. And only then, because I know I'll have to. I can't keep you and hold you forever, but for tonight, I don't want to take my hands off you. Or my mouth," he whispered, kissing away her answer.

His kiss was possessive, demanding, and she returned his kiss passionately and clung to him. They stood in each other's arms and she ran her hands over his shoulders and nape while one leg rose up to pull him even closer. His deep moan thrilled her, because it meant she had excited him as he had her. Knowing that, she burned with need, wanting his hands and mouth and body all over hers.

As she started to put her foot down, he caught her leg, holding it and sliding his hand up along her calf, over her knee, going higher till he touched her intimately and she gasped as his fingers rubbed and caressed her.

Her breath was coming in short bursts when he finally picked her up. "A bed?"

She pointed behind her and pulled his head down to kiss him, needing the contact as he carried her through the condo to set her on her feet beside her bed. He yanked back the covers and placed her on the bed, coming down beside her to pull her into his arms and continue kissing her.

He was hard muscle, warm against her, and she ran her hand over his marvelous body. Minutes later, he moved to her feet, holding her foot and watching her, while he trailed his tongue across her ankle and along her leg. His fingers caressed her leg, sliding slowly, so lightly up her leg and the back of her thigh, barely touching her.

He showered kisses on her leg, rolling her over on her stomach to caress the back of her thighs and run his tongue over her. She moaned softly and in minutes turned over again as his hands drifted to the inside of her thighs while he leaned down to kiss her, his tongue touching hers. She wrapped her arms around his neck, holding him, kissing him in return until he moved back, letting his tongue slide down her front, circling each nipple and then moving lower, his mouth joining his hands where they played between her thighs.

Crying out, she arched, raising her hips, giving him more access to her while he stroked her intimately, gently at first then with more pressure, his fingers and tongue taking her near the pinnacle. But she didn't want the pleasure to end.

With a cry she sat up and pushed him back on the bed, moving over him to stroke his manhood, to tease and pleasure him as he had her. She ran her tongue, hot and wet, over him in long, slow strokes until he reached down to lift her back on the bed where he could move between her legs.

She held his hips. "Love me, now, Mike. I want you inside me. I want your hardness, your body and mouth on me."

"Not yet, darlin'," he whispered, kissing her throat while his fingers toyed intimately with her and then he moved down to kiss her, his tongue stroking where his fingers just been, making her cry out and spread her legs for him to have total access.

He knelt between her legs, leaning down, his tongue going over her as much as his fingers while she writhed with desire. Her hands drifted over him to grasp his shoulders to draw him to her. "Mike, come here," she whispered.

He kissed her as he moved up until he stretched out beside her, his hands still toying with her, exciting her, and her hands seeking out and holding his thick rod.

"I can't wait any longer," she cried as she straddled him.

"Yes, you can. You wanted me to make love to you for a long time tonight. You told me that, so that's what we'll do." He rolled her over so he was on top, laving her nipples as his roaming fingers found a home in her most intimate place. "Let's make this last. This is good, Vivian, so good."

But she couldn't withstand any more of the tender onslaught. She gripped his shoulders, arching her back and thrusting her hips against him. "Mike,

I want you now. I need you inside me. I want to love you and I want you to make love to me."

He stepped off the bed to get his billfold and took out a packet. In minutes, he knelt between her legs as he put on the condom and lowered himself, easing into her. She gasped, raising her hips for him while she wrapped her long legs around him.

He moved slowly, his hard rod teasing her and heightening her desire with each thrust. She wanted him desperately, wanted more each time he entered her and withdrew, and she moved with his rhythm, arching her back and locking her legs more tightly around him.

"Mike, I want you," she whispered, running her hands over him. Her eyes were squeezed shut, her whole world was focused on moving with him, on the sensations rocking her. He withdrew slowly and she felt bereft, empty, until he plunged deeply into her and then pumped hard and fast. She kept pace with him as need drove her, until she reached the point of no return. When her release burst over her, she cried out and shuddered. Yet she moved with him, faster than ever, ecstasy streaking through her with each thrust of her hips, her climax shattering, fulfilling needs and dreams. She cried out, turning her head to kiss his shoulder while he pumped frantically and then his climax came.

They slowed, both gasping for breath. She held him tightly as rapture enveloped her, a happiness that she hadn't felt in a long time. She kissed his jaw, and he turned his head, moving on his side and keeping her with him. She kissed him lightly, showering kisses over his ear. "You sexy man," she whispered.

He smiled while he toyed with long locks of her hair. "Darlin', you absolutely hands-down win the prize for being the most sexy possible. I don't think I can move again."

"Mike, this is such a special time in my life. Tonight is filled with fun, laughter, red hot sex, dancing, partying, being together, wild pleasure—a heap of fabulous things that all add up to happiness. Tonight was the happiest night I've had in so long."

"Ah, Vivian, this is just a tough time. We all have that. You'll move on and times will be good again."

"You're an optimist, too."

He shifted slightly to look at her. "What's this 'too' business? What else am I?"

"Definitely, you're thoroughly an al—"

"—pha male," he finished for her. "Well, let me tell you, sweetie, you better keep hiring alpha males to run this ranch."

She twisted to look more closely at him. "You're not here to stay? Forever?"

He smiled at her. "Let's not let life intrude. Think about the past hour instead of the future. I could spend the rest of the night thinking about the past hour," he said, rolling over on his back and placing his hand behind his head, to prop his head up slightly.

She shifted and rested her chin on her palm to look down at him.

"You're serious. You're not keeping this job forever."

"Darlin'. I must not have carried you out of this world tonight. You're back worrying about the ranch."

She stared at him a moment and knew her suspicions were correct that he would quit and move on after he had fulfilled what he felt he needed to for Thane. She should be so much more cautious or he would give her another terrible heartbreak on top of losing Thane. She stopped all thoughts of his job or the ranch and instead thought about his kisses and his hands moving on her. She nuzzled his neck. "You're right," she said softly. "The last hour has been wonderful. Definitely. And I will think about it over and over because every moment was fabulous, sensuous and exciting."

"That's better. That's good to hear as a matter of fact. That makes me think we might have an encore. In a few more minutes, of course."

He turned on his side and they gazed at each other. She smiled and he touched the raised corner of her lips lightly with his index finger. "You're beautiful, Vivian. Absolutely, totally beautiful."

She loved hearing the compliment and gave him one in return. "Mike, tonight was wonderful. The dinner, the dancing, the loving, the company were everything I wanted, everything I dreamed about and longed for. You're too sexy for words."

"Good, darlin'. I want you happy." He ran his hand over her shoulder, down her back and over her bottom. "You have the softest, smoothest skin in the entire US of A."

They looked at each other and both smiled. She ran her finger along his jaw, feeling the short bristly stubble. "A sexy man, so rugged, so handsome. You know, you could be a model."

He laughed. "I don't think so, but you can keep thinking that. Now in reality, you are the model type. Maybe a few more delightful curves on you than some, thank goodness." His smile vanished. "It was good, Vivian. A really good night. You're a wonderful woman."

She laughed and rose up slightly to brush his cheek with a kiss. "I suppose you're my knight in shining armor."

"Oh, no. I'm just a Texas cowboy." He pulled her into the crook of his arm, tightly pressed against his side. "This is paradise," he said, and she felt the vibration in his chest when he talked.

"We should talk about you moving in to the main house. You should come check out the suite and make arrangements for help to bring over your things." She halted his reply with her finger on his lips. "I know, you don't have much."

"Vivian, I think we should stick to just talking about tonight, making love, your fabulous body, the past hour, what fun it was to dance tonight, and keep all that other stuff out of the bedroom. We'll have a whole lot more fun and we won't get into anything serious, disturbing or worrisome. Do you agree?"

She laughed. "Tell me that again."

"You heard me and you know what I said."

"I surely do. We can leave off my fabulous body

because you have the fab body, dear sir," she said, squeezing a bicep. "Oh, my. That makes my heart go pitter-patter."

"Let me feel and see," he said, placing his hand lightly on her breast. She laughed and rolled over to look at him.

"By the way, I have a fabulous shower and tub," she said, pointing past him to her en suite.

"Let's try them out," he said, stepping off the bed and leaning over to scoop her up in his arms.

"Oh, my. See, I told you that you have fabulous muscles."

"You're a featherweight. Did you know that I haven't even seen your condo? Not only that, this place has all glass walls and we're naked. Are we on display for the world?"

"No, we're not. They can't see in. We can see out."

He peered out the window. "If I'm not mistaken, there's a balcony all around this place."

"That's correct. A rather large balcony with a swimming pool."

He continued to the bathroom.

"Here's the light switch," she said, reaching out to the wall and flipping it on.

He looked around a large room with palm trees in pots, a chaise lounge in deep red and purple throw rugs on a marble floor. Along with the recessed lighting she had also switched on music at a control panel and a soft tune emanated from hidden speakers. He carried her over to the raised tub; set high on three steps. It was a large marble bath with gold fixtures. He had a feeling they were real gold.

She punched more buttons and water splashed into the tub. "At this point, I suggest you put me down and I'll check on the water."

"How about turning that off and let's try the shower."

"Sure," she said and pointed to a large glassed-in shower at the other side of the bathroom.

They showered together and in minutes he picked her up, stepped out of the spray and let her slide down on his hard manhood while he kissed her. She wrapped her legs around him, moving with him, holding him tightly while his thrusts came hard and fast until they climaxed together. She cried out in ecstasy, holding him tightly, tilting his head up to kiss him. She slid down the length of his body and finally put her feet on the floor. She looked up to see him smile at her as he ran his fingers through her hair, pushing it back from her face.

"You're marvelous, Vivian. Hot, sexy. Let's try that shower again."

"This time let's make it back to the bed."

He laughed as they showered together and then dried each other. He picked her up again to carry her to bed, stretching out and holding her close against him.

"I want you in my arms tonight."

"I'm not arguing with that," she said, snuggling against him. She was happy and he was right when he said she shouldn't think beyond the present hour, but it was hard not to. The night had been fabulous, a temporary fix for loneliness and losing Thane, and it would help for a long time. The hot sex they'd shared would drive away some of her demons, be a lasting memory she could pull out that wouldn't hold so much sadness and longing.

She and Mike weren't in love with each other. But she had a feeling if he came around as much in the coming months as he had been since he started working for her, she could fall in love with him. He'd told her not to think of the future, but it was impossible not to.

She looked at him and wondered if he was asleep or just lying there holding her.

She didn't want to fall in love with him because he would never ever return it. He would never get past that damn stubborn view of her fortune. She didn't even think it was a woman boss that bothered him. It was a woman-billionaire boss. He had been a total gentleman with Marta at the gallery and he hadn't displayed any dismay when he reported to Vivian on the ranch. He hadn't even cared this time when she picked up the tab at the club. It was her inheritance that he couldn't deal with. That and some miguided loyalty to Thane who was gone and would never be part of her life. Thane wanted Mike to take his place. She was beginning to suspect Thane hoped she and Mike would fall in love. Thane loved the ranch and probably thought once Mike was here, he would stay.

She was sure he wouldn't. Also, Thane must not have known how strongly Mike felt about a very wealthy woman. How could someone object to money? She rose up to look at him.

"What?" he asked without opening his eyes.

"I thought you were asleep."

"Just about."

"You haven't even opened your eyes."

He opened them to look at her. "What are you worrying about?"

"Are you an incredibly light sleeper or were you just lying there with your eyes closed?"

"A little of both. Probably the military life and being in places where you could get killed if you didn't wake up easily." He held out his arms and she scooted down against him.

"Mmm, I like this. This is good," he said quietly, running his hand over her breast.

She inhaled. "I don't think you're going back to sleep."

He turned on his side. "I don't think so either," he said in a husky voice. He pulled her closer to kiss her. She slipped one arm around him to hold him close as she shut her eyes and kissed him in return.

It was over two hours later when she lay in the dark trying once again to go to sleep. He was an incredibly light sleeper and if he woke up again, she suspected they would make love once more. Her body ached in places she had forgotten even existed.

What would happen when they returned to the ranch? She guessed life would go right back to like it had been before even if he was just down the hall and no one else was in that wing. Would he treat this night as if it had never happened?

Six

Mike turned to her, placing his palm against her cheek. "What's worrying you, Vivian? Is it Thane?"

"Thane?" she asked in surprise. "Not at all. Thane's gone, Mike, and he's never coming back to me. I keep saying it—he would want me to go on with my life. I know that for certain."

"You're right about that," Mike said, caressing her cheek and then playing with a long lock of her hair. "He would want you to, just as you would want him to if something had happened to you. So what is it?"

"I just don't understand your attitude about my inheritance."

There was a long moment of silence.

"If I didn't have that kind of income and inheritance, you would date me after tonight, wouldn't you?" she asked.

"I probably would, but there's no way to think about you without your inheritance because it exists and it isn't going away. I can't deal with that, Vivian. Maybe it was because of growing up without much, but there's no way I can go out with a woman who has inherited millions from her husband and is heir to a man worth billions. I was raised to feel that a man who relies on a woman for money isn't really a man. Before my aunt divorced my uncle, she offered to give dad money to pay when my youngest brother was born. I can still remember that fight and my dad wouldn't take a penny. It might not have been smart, but that's just the way I am."

She sat up and pulled the sheet up beneath her arms. "I have never known anyone who objected to money."

"I don't object to money. I'd be happy to have a bunch, but not from the woman I love. I'd feel like a kept man. I'd feel like I couldn't be myself, argue about anything. You'll never understand, because you were born into that and you've lived with it all your life. It's your family and your family money. It has belonged to you since the day you were born." He tunneled his fingers through his hair and blew out a breath. "You may not be able to understand how I feel but my feelings are real. My dad had strong feelings about it and taught his sons that the man should pay, the man should have the money. Also, his brother married a wealthy woman, and they fought over everything and she was snippy when she would come to our house. She would leave my mom in tears about what a dump we lived in. It was home and we liked it. They finally divorced, but she caused some hard feelings and bad times. As a kid there were times I've gone hungry rather than have some woman who wasn't related, buy my dinner. The year dad died was bad and we did go to bed hungry. I had a teacher who would try to buy my lunch and I just couldn't let her do it. That's just how I was brought up. So, no, we can't date. I don't want to fall in love with a woman worth billions. What could I ever buy for you that would thrill you, surprise you? Impossible."

"Can you hear yourself and what you're saying?"

"Damn well can and it makes sense to me. I told you to avoid thinking about life back at the ranch and about tomorrow, to just stick with tonight." He pulled her down on his chest. "Darlin', don't you ever get sleepy?"

She sat up again and poked his chest lightly with her finger. "You're an alpha male who can't let a woman pay your way. You're archaic—from another century."

"Hell yes, I'm old-fashioned. I can't deal with a woman who is a billionaire when I make a very measly salary in comparison."

"Are you through?"

"Absolutely."

"Life is more than money in the bank."

"It sure as hell isn't when you're starving."

"Don't give me that. You may have had a tough childhood, but you've done well. Not like my dad, no. But you've done well and you're a damn good rancher."

"Dammit, Vivian. I'm tired of hearing about that. I am what I am. Let's just go from there and I'll do what alpha males do. Come here." He pulled her into his arms and kissed her.

She opened her mouth to object and pushed against his chest, her anger rising, but he tightened his arm around her while his mouth covered her protest and his tongue went deep. Despite his plundering lips, his touch was gentle. He caressed her breast, so lightly, a feather touch that made her tremble, and all her anger disappeared. She moaned in response, wanting his caresses, wanting him as she held his wrist and kept his hand on her breast. She wanted his loving, his hot, passionate kisses that were possessive this time, his sexy tongue stroking hers, touching the corners of her mouth, teasing and tormenting and making her crave him desperately.

She wrapped her arms around his neck and rubbed her bare breasts against his chest, shifting and straddling him as they both sat in bed and continued to kiss. The conflicting emotions of anger and desire drove her to want to kiss him until he wouldn't be able to walk away so easily. If he just wasn't so stubborn, they could have something good together.

She stopped thinking because she was lost in his fiery kiss. Suddenly he rolled her over and he was on top, moving over her and looking down at her. Gone was the anger she'd heard in his voice. His green eyes were dark with lust. He looked at her as if she were the most desirable woman he had ever encountered. Her heart thudded as she looked up at him and felt as if he wanted her more than anyone else on earth.

His hands caressed her breasts lightly, slowly while he shifted, moving down so he could kiss her breasts. His lovemaking was possessive and erotic, driving her wild. "Mike, love me," she whispered, kissing his throat, stroking his manhood rising up to run her tongue over him.

He turned her, pulling her up to kiss her again— another kiss that melted her.

He entered her then withdrew, teasing, making her want him beyond anything she'd felt earlier. Finally, he eased into her and let go of his iron control and then pumped wildly, each thrust going deeper inside her. She cried out with her climax. And then still driven, she had the second climax with his, gasping and holding him as they both reached ecstasy.

It seemed hours before her heartbeat and her breathing were normal. She clung to him, holding him tightly, wondering if she had made a huge mistake tonight. She didn't want to fall in love with him and she feared making love to him tonight had just brought her closer to him, made him more important to her.

She needed to go back to the ranch and not see Mike for a while unless she had to for business. Too late for that, she realized. He was moving into her house, on her floor, down the hall from her suite.

He pulled her close against him. "That was fantastic, darlin'. That's one place we don't have an argument in the world. You're incredibly sexy."

She held him tightly in silence, wondering how much he had captured her heart tonight. She wondered if he would quit working at the ranch when the three months he had promised Thane were up. She knew he wouldn't go and leave her in the lurch. He'd, stay till she hired someone and he trained the person. Suddenly, she was certain that that was exactly what he would do and probably what he had planned all along. The more she thought about it, the more certain she was that she was right.

Thane was gone. Slade would soon be gone and then Mike would eventually leave, as well. There would be absolutely nothing to hold her at the ranch. Thane's dad didn't like the ranch. His grandfather was no longer living. And she and Thane had no children, no heirs. Thane always said he was the only one in his family now who wanted to be a rancher.

Why would she stay on the ranch? She shook her head. The Tumbling T would be filled with memories that would hurt too much.

Mike turned, shifting to look at her. "This has been a special night, Vivian. Come here," he said, pulling her against his side with his arm around her. "Try to get some sleep. We've been awake the entire night and it's getting so late that we'll see the sun come up soon. Stop worrying about my attitude. You and I aren't in love. We've had a wonderful time together and that was a gift for me and I hope one for you. I promise you, Vivian, your life will be happy. You'll never miss me being in it."

She snuggled against him, holding him tightly, seizing the moment and temporarily letting go of all her worries. For the next hour, she wasn't going to think about tomorrow or telling him goodbye or anything else except his marvelous body, the feel of his arms around her and this night of loving that had been hot, sexy and joyous. The more she thought about his lovemaking, his hands and mouth and hard muscular body, the more aroused she was until she shifted slightly and ran her tongue along his ear. She heard and felt his deep breath as his arm tightened around her and he caressed her breast.

It took no time to arouse him. After putting on a condom, he lifted her on top of him and eased slowly inside her, filling her. She moaned, relishing his hard rod.

He thrust into her, going faster, until she was wild with passion, riding him as her climax burst with hot pleasure that set her body ablaze. He continued and she could feel another climax coming. This time they moved together and she cried out as rapture spilled over her.

She showered kisses on his throat, his ear, his mouth, holding him and then sliding off him to lie beside him again. He turned on his side, pulling her close and brushing strands of hair away from her face.

"It's good, Vivian. So very good together."

When their breathing returned to normal, he

picked her up and carried her to the en suite where he ran hot water into the big tub and sank down, holding her on his lap. She wiggled her bottom and he chuckled. "You haven't had enough yet?"

She twisted to caress and kiss him. "You adorable, sexy man. I still want you to make love to me, but let's sit here and talk a few minutes then dry off and get back in a bed."

"That's a plan because this is a fine moment right now." He ran his hands over her, covering her breasts and belly, sliding down her legs and up her back. "Every inch of you is sexy, sleek, soft and beautiful and I want to touch you everywhere, to excite you again."

She leaned back against him while he wrapped both arms around her waist to hold her. "Now relax and tell me about your life. Tell me things I don't know. Tell me things you want in life," she said.

"I want you and I want to make love to you for several more hours. As for what I want in life—I can't think past this night. This is fabulous, Vivian."

After a few minutes, he stood and stepped out of the tub and helped her up, grabbing a towel to dry her off while she ran another towel over his exciting, masculine body.

"I think the sun has come up, Mike. We haven't slept at all. It's Saturday."

"So it is."

Tingling, wanting to kiss him, she turned and looked up at him. "I have an appointment at eleven o'clock to take some frames to be repaired."

"Call them and postpone it. Tell them something urgent has come up. And that's the truth," he said, rubbing his thick rod against her thigh while he nibbled her ear.

She turned her head to kiss him as she wound her arm around his neck. "I bet you have to get back, too."

"Not so, darlin'. I'll send a text when I get time," he said, nuzzling her neck. "I want to stay right here in your plush, ritzy condo on top of the world, at least our corner of it, and make love all day long."

"That is so decadent."

"You wanted to have a life again. You wanted laughter, sex and fun. Here it is, just waiting for you."

She laughed. "You're wicked, Mike Moretti. And you are the most fun I've had in a long time. When you put it that way—" She held out both hands. "On one hand, I can get my picture frames fixed. On the other, I can have raging, blazing sex with you." She twisted to look into his eyes. "I do believe you win out."

"That makes me feel really important. And sexy. I beat the picture frame repair."

"Mike, you do better than that," she said, brushing a light kiss on his mouth.

His smile vanished and desire filled his expression. "I want you as if we haven't made love ever. I want you now, Vivian." He picked her up to carry her back to bed, holding her close as he kissed her.

The sun was low in the western sky when she sat up cross-legged in bed, pulled the sheet beneath her arms and poked his shoulder with her finger. "Listen to me. From the first few minutes we came here after leaving the club last night, we have either been in bed or in the shower or in my tub. It is almost night again. We haven't eaten and my stomach is protesting. This is super-decadent. I haven't had clothes on since yesterday."

"I find that an absolutely terrific argument to continue what we've been doing. Is there any way to get food up here to you besides dropping a basket on a rope over the balcony?"

"Of course, although it hasn't come up before. I'm not here a lot and when I am, I've planned ahead more than I did this time. I thought we'd be up and out of here by nine this morning. I didn't realize how lusty and sex-starved you were."

"I see several choices here—we dress and I take you out to eat. The drawback to that one is for about two hours we will have to wear clothes. I won't be able to touch you where and when I want to touch you. I won't be able to kiss you, bathe with you or do fun things with you. Eating with you is way down that list.

"Another choice is to call in and have something delivered. That means clothes for about an hour while we wait for the delivery and going down to get the stuff. Much better choice to my way of thinking.

"Or, send me out. There are hotels around us. For a little extra, I'll bet I can get an adequate meal in a jiffy and get back here."

"Remember, you don't have a car."

"That doesn't matter. There are probably two hotels on this block and I'm fast."

"I'll bet you are when you think there's a naked lady waiting in your bed," she said, smiling at him and he smiled in return.

"I vote for choice three," he said after feigning serious contemplation. "Now I can come up with a fourth choice, but I don't think you'll want it. Just eat tomorrow. To get to stay naked and in bed with you, I can go that route easily."

"That's because of your ranger training. You could go until Tuesday if you had to. But for me that choice is out. I haven't had any ranger training and I'm hungry for some real food."

"Darlin', why didn't you stock the fridge up here?"

"I didn't think we'd be here long."

"That is an amazing lack of foresight. Okay, choice number three it is. Send me out. I'm efficient, fast and you get a little bonus or two if I do this."

She leaned closer. "So what is this wonderful bonus? Am I going to be interested?"

"I think so. I will give you a wonderful, relaxing massage before we have sex."

She laughed. "You don't know one thing about giving a massage."

He grinned. "You have no idea what I all know. Try me and see. I promise you won't be disappointed."

"Just go get us something to eat. I'm not particular about what it is. I just want food."

"Breakfast, lunch or dinner kind of food?"

"I better have a steak so I can keep up my strength. I need it with you. I haven't been working out every day for the past few years the way you have."

"You are in absolutely perfect shape, sweetie. You couldn't be in any better shape."

She smiled at him. "Thank you." She held the sheet as she stepped out of bed. "Now, you get going before I faint from hunger."

"For such a dainty little thing, you have such a big appetite."

"I've been busy," she teased.

"Well, rest up, darlin', you'll be busy when I get back with the steaks."

"I hope that's a promise," she said in a sultry voice, flirting with him and having fun doing it.

He wrapped his arms around her and kissed her—a long, steamy kiss. When he finally stopped, she opened her eyes to find him gazing at her. "That was definitely a promise," he said in a husky voice. "I'm going to set a speed record for getting you a steak and getting back here."

She nodded. She wanted him and if he had wanted to go back to bed right now, she wouldn't have protested. Her night of reckless lovemaking had spilled into another day and she couldn't be happier. She'd relish it right up until they had to leave.

The following Thursday, Mike came for dinner and while Francie got the meal ready with Henry's help, Vivian greeted Mike at the door.

Vivian had spent an hour dressing and changing before she was satisfied with a short-sleeved red linen blouse and slacks with high-heeled sandals. When Mike walked in the door, he gave her his hat and followed her into the study. As he walked toward her, her breathing quickened. He looked more handsome than ever. He wore a white dress shirt under his tan jacket and dark brown slacks with brown boots. His black hair was slightly windblown over his forehead.

"Do you want the house tour now or after dinner?" she asked him.

"Definitely now. I'd hate to get lost in this place."

"It's not that big."

"Would you like a drink before we start the tour?"

"Oh, yeah. That would be nice." He crossed the room to her. "We're being mighty formal when you think about the last time we were together. And let me tell you now—you look beautiful."

She felt her cheeks grow warm. "Thank you for the compliment. As for your greeting—you surely didn't expect me to throw myself into your arms, did you?"

"I might have hoped. This isn't a bad substitute," he said, wrapping his arms around her and leaning forward to brush his lips on hers.

She couldn't protest. Her heartbeat quickened, even faster than when she'd first seen him come in the door looking so handsome and strong and sexy, reminding her of being naked in his arms.

When he released her, she looked up at him and

felt dazed. "Wow. You'll make me forget dinner and Francie has cooked all afternoon."

"I'm not going to hurt her feelings, but I'll tell you, Vivian, I could ditch the best dinner on earth for your kisses."

"That's very flattering, Mike. Am I going to be able to let you move into my house? We can't stay in bed together. We aren't moving into the same bed-room."

"I'll work on that one. I'd like to see these rooms we're talking about. Beer first, though."

"I'll do that, but right now, let's cover the big news of the day. I imagine you already know it because he said he was going to talk to you next. Slade came by with his resignation."

"I know. He told me. I'm glad for him, putting any feelings I have aside. His back bothers him and he shouldn't be doing what he does. He said he gave you a two-week notice."

"He did. I told him he doesn't have to wait two weeks. We all will miss him, but you're right. His family is in south Texas and they want him with them and he wants to go. I think he'll go a little sooner than two weeks."

"I told him we'd help him any way we can," Mike said and she nodded.

"I told him we'd have a party. He said it's not nec-essary, but we will. Maybe next Tuesday night if the guys are okay with it. You see what night might be best. We'll have a barbeque if it's good weather. Also,

congratulations, Mike. You'll officially become foreman when he leaves and your salary will go up."

"Thank you," he said, smiling at her.

"Now I'll see about our drinks and the tour. I'll
be right back." She left and in less than a minute she
was back, followed by Henry who had a tray with a
cold, open beer, a bowl of pretzels and a glass of iced
tea. He held out the glass to Vivian and went to Mike.

"Would you like a cold beer?"

"Oh, would I ever. Thanks, Henry. I'd set the pretzels close by, too."

When they were alone, he sipped his beer, lowered
the bottle and looked at her. "Now, I think you were
going to show me around before dinner."

"Then we'll get to it. The third floor has suites
where Henry and Millie live, and Francie lives on
that floor, too. Heather and Waldo also live on the
third floor. In short, we stay off the third floor. I have
a suite on the second floor. That's where you'll be.
They don't come on the second floor. We don't go to
the third floor. Now, in the basement is a wine cel-
lar, a storage area and another library for the kind of
papers and stuff that would look junky in the main
library." She stopped when she heard him chuckle.
"Why are you laughing?"

"You live in what's half museum and half hotel.
Holy saints, where is an ordinary room?"

"You're standing in one and there are plenty of
ordinary rooms," she said, thinking his smile and
laughter were irresistible. She could detect a faint
scent of aftershave and when she looked at his broad

shoulders, all she could think about was last weekend and how those shoulders felt beneath her hands
when they were both naked.

He looked around. "It's difficult to think of this as
Thane's home. He was practical and sort of a mini-
malist."

"That was his military persona. Otherwise, you're
wrong there. He lived all over the place here. In the
gym with an indoor pool. In the ballroom. Even in
the indoor tennis court down in the basement."

He waved her off. "Show me where I'll sleep and
come in and go out, and where you sleep and where
I'll eat. That's enough of a tour for me."

"I'm beginning to wonder about you," she said.

"And what are you wondering?"

"You sound as if you live under a bridge." She
shook her head at him then continued the tour. "You
know where the garage is. You can come in the back
like you did tonight. We'll go up these stairs. There's
a back staircase, too and separate elevators to the
second and third floors. The elevator's handy when
they move furniture, times like that, but I never take
it." She walked with Mike up the sweeping spiral
staircase in the front hall and she stopped in the
center of a wide second-floor hallway. "To the right
is my suite," she said, pointing. "To the left will be
your suite. Let's go look. We'll be the only ones living on this floor."

"I can't wait," he said, sipping his beer. "Are you
sure this house wasn't your idea? This doesn't look
like something Thane would have built."

"The house I grew up in is a two-story frame and brick house with five bedrooms, six bathrooms, a three-car garage, a great room, a family room, a dining room and a kitchen. Nothing like this. I think Thane had ideas we would fill it with people and kids but that isn't ever going to happen now."

They walked down the hall to double doors that were open. She stepped inside and he followed her into what would be his suite, starting with a living area with floor-to-ceiling windows and glass doors that slid open on to a wide balcony.

"It's beautiful," he said. His voice had changed and he set his beer on a table as he turned to her. "Now that we're alone, it's time for what's really important," he said, slipping his arms around her waist and leaning down to kiss her.

She couldn't say no. Her heart missed beats as she wound her arms around his neck, stood on tiptoe and kissed him in return. She moaned softly, pleased to be back in his arms.

"Tell the staff to go home soon. I don't care if I ever eat. I want you, Vivian. I want you in my arms."

She clung to him, kissing him, knowing she was going to have giant regrets, yet she couldn't stop. All week she had dreamed about him, about his kisses, about his arms around her, holding her tightly. She ran her hands over him as they kissed.

"Which room do we sleep in tonight? In here? In yours?"

"Mike, we're going to get hurt."

"I can't say we won't. But that doesn't stop me from wanting you."

They kissed and conversation ended temporarily. Finally, she raised her head. "I didn't ask you to move into my bedroom."

"Okay, we can move—"

"No, we're not moving in here."

"Fine. You and I know how to walk down a hall. That's what we'll do. You can't tell me you don't want this," he said, his mouth covering any answer she might have had.

She knew this was folly and she was headed straight for heartbreak. He would never change and all too soon he would leave the Tumbling T and tell her goodbye, but she couldn't resist when he was kissing her senseless and she couldn't deny that she wanted him to. She didn't want dinner and she doubted if he did, but they'd have to go eat and then come back upstairs where they could be alone.

"Mike, let's go sit downstairs and make some semblance of having dinner and spending the evening together without going to bed."

She wasn't sure if her words were getting through to him. He seemed intent on running his fingers along her cheek, his eyes never leaving her. "So soft," he whispered. Then he looked up at her. "All right. We'll go downstairs for a while. How soon will the house empty out of the other residents?"

"About half an hour after dinner," she said. "So we might as well go ahead and eat something."

He nodded. "This takes great restraint. I've

thought about you all day long and wanted you in my arms. I dream about you at night."

"Mike, asking you to move here wasn't an invitation to move into my bed."

He caught her chin with his hand, bent his knees so he was on her level and could look directly into her eyes. "You don't want to make love tonight?"

"You know I do and I can't resist you, but that isn't smart and that is not why I wanted you to move in here."

"I'll do what you want. I'll sleep in my bed and leave you alone to sleep in yours if that's what you want. But the least you can do is let me kiss you and squeeze you and—"

She backed up. "You're not paying attention. We should avoid all that physical stuff if we want to avoid a boatload of hurt. You've seen where you sleep and you know where I sleep. We'll have lots of time after dinner. Right now while Francie is getting dinner on and Henry is underfoot, let's go back downstairs and sit and talk until we're called to dinner."

"Fine, Vivian. I'll act as if I have little interest in you or your luscious, sexy body."

She threw up her hands. "I give up."

He moved closer to talk softly in her ear. "You, my darlin', love sex, love making love and you are as eager as I am when the opportunity arises. During dinner, it won't hurt for you to go ahead and think about kisses afterward."

"Mike, you are shameless," she said, but she tingled and wanted to be in his arms, and she couldn't

stop thinking about kissing him later. She wanted
more from him while at the same time she knew that
wasn't going to happen and she should treat their affair as lightly as he was because she hadn't wanted
to fall in love with him. That would mean rushing
straight into more hurt and another broken heart.
He didn't want anything from her except sex and
she was already getting a heartache over him. Had
she already fallen in love with him? She hoped not.

As they left the suite, she asked about his day.

"I have some news—Leon turned in his resignation, so he is out of your life for good. He's got a
job on a horse ranch in southwest Texas. Everyone
wished him well. His last day is next week. I doubt
if he'll come say goodbye, but if he does and you
want me around, just call. I have an idea that this
may end Clint's information source on where you
are, but that's a guess on my part."

"I'm glad he has a good job offer and he'll be gone
soon. It's wonderful news. I think your moving in
here will take care of my neighbor, too."

"Your problems are solved," he said.

"No, they're not," she said. "But Leon leaving
and you moving in take care of two big ones that I
needed help to handle."

He stood looking at her and she tilted her head.
"What?"

"You look beautiful, Vivian," he said solemnly.

"Thank you," she answered, wondering what
was bothering him because he looked worried. "We
should go down for dinner."

"You're right." He walked downstairs beside her without taking her arm, which she found unusual. Was he thinking about Thane? She didn't know Mike well enough to guess what made him so somber all of a sudden so she decided just to ask.

"What's wrong, Mike?"

He turned to meet her questioning gaze. "You are an observant one, aren't you? Actually, I was thinking about us. I don't want to hurt you ever, Vivian."

She smiled and patted his hand. "I don't want to hurt you, either. Maybe we both should use a little more restraint and caution. After all, you may disappear out of my life when your three months are over. If I'm not careful, you could say goodbye and go, taking my heart with you. I can't go through that after losing Thane."

"We're not that serious, Vivian."

"You're not. And I'm not yet. Besides, you're never going to change, Mike."

"Don't tell me again that I'm an alpha male. I know that's how you see me."

"They don't change to beta males or whatever the other kind is—the ones who don't have to run the show and be top dog."

He leaned close to whisper, "We're fun in bed."

She pushed him away. "You have a one-track mind."

When they got downstairs, Henry told them their dinner would be served out on the patio where they could enjoy the warm spring evening. Mike held her chair out and then sat facing her. Gone was his solemn expression, replaced by a cheerful smile and a positive attitude as he talked about the ranch.

Mike ate heartily, clearly enjoying his meal. As he cut into his meat, he smiled at Vivian. "You're right. Francie can cook. This meat is delicious—our own and so tender I can cut it with my fork. The veggies are from the ranch, too, aren't they? The greenhouses help, but this is asparagus season and steamed asparagus from the garden can't be beat."

"I agree, Mike. Francie is a great cook. She's widowed but she dates Merrick, one of the cowhands who work for you. I expect them to marry one day and I hope I don't lose her."

After a few minutes, Vivian sipped her water and placed the glass on the table while she looked at Mike. "You told me about your family, Mike. A little bit about them. Where are they now?"

"In Amarillo, Texas. Mom didn't finish a high school education and she had four boys. We're all scattered now but we take care of Mom. We've bought her a house, have someone to clean for her, someone to take care of the yard. She has lots of friends and has a church group. She's happy and she's seems to be doing okay."

"That's good."

"She took care of us. Now we take care of her. It's a simple equation, but a lot of people don't get it."

Vivian and Mike both passed on dessert and moved inside to the family room to get out of Francie's way while she cleaned up the patio table.

"My things are in the pickup," Mike told her after a while. "Maybe I should take them in now."

"Go get your stuff moved so you and I can kiss."

"Now you have my full attention and cooperation."

It was fun having him around. But she admitted the truth to herself. She was falling in love with him and she knew he would not return it. He was not in love with her and he never would be unless her family lost their fortune.

"Stubborn, stubborn man," she whispered, hurting because Mike was so many great things, so capable, kind, brave, funny—but so old-fashioned. That always came up, each time she was with him. She knew he was well-fixed for himself and cared for his mother financially. Other than that, she didn't know how much money he had, but it wasn't an issue for her. She sighed. How could she have fallen in love with someone so difficult?

Tonight, was she going to be in his bed? Or Mike in hers? She knew the answer. It was just another link in the chain that would bind her heart to him. He would never fall in love with her. All he could see was her financial worth, which to him translated to power. And that went against everything he was—something he made her aware of every time they were together.

She got up to see if she could help Francie finish so the woman could retire for the night. Francie was still putting things away and Vivian began to help in spite of her protests.

"You'll be through and then you can go. Thanks for dinner. It was delicious as always."

"Thank you."

After a few minutes, they finished and Francie told her good-night, leaving for her suite on the third floor.

Vivian walked upstairs to see how Mike was doing and met Mike at the top of the stairs. "I was just coming to see how you are doing."

"Henry helped and we're finished moving me in."

"You do travel light. That didn't take any time at all."

"No, darlin', and that gives me a lot more time for you. Henry has gone to make some outdoor rounds and then he'll go home, which I suppose means the third floor. In the meantime, let's go try out my new digs. I'll bet you've never spent the night there."

"Henry takes care of locking up the house and setting the alarms every night. But just in case of an emergency, I'll show you how to do it. I can do it from up here," she said. "See that little box?" She started to turn to point, but his arm wrapped around her waist.

"There is only one thing I can see, and that is you. I've waited for this moment for almost a week now. I want you, Vivian. You look sexy and beautiful tonight. You just take my breath away when I look at you."

She gazed into his eyes that had darkened as they always did when he was aroused. The look he gave her made her heart beat faster. She wanted his kisses and wanted his arms around her, holding her against his heart. She wanted to hold him and try to avoid the knowledge that she couldn't hold him long. He would always leave her and someday he wouldn't return and she was going to have another big heartache. She knew all that, but she was determined to grab all the happiness she could...for as long as she could.

He kissed her, his tongue touching hers, ending her worries, making her forget everything except Mike and his lovemaking.

While he still kissed her, he picked her up to carry her to his bedroom. There was only a sheet on the bed, but she didn't care as he stood her on her feet again.

He wound his fingers in her hair. "I haven't slept for thinking about you, for wanting you," he said gruffly, looking into her eyes.

"Vivian, I want to kiss and make love to you all night long," he whispered while his hands moved over her. He peeled away her red blouse, tossing it aside as she unfastened the buttons of his cotton shirt. Soon all their clothing was gone and he picked her up to kiss her. She wrapped her long legs around him, holding him tightly as he moved to the bed and laid her down. He left her only long enough to sheath himself in a condom and then returned to her. Lifting her astride him, he filled her with his manhood.

He caressed her breasts while she moved on him, his thumbs circling her nipples as he thrust into her. She set the pace, riding him faster, her hair flying across her shoulders. Her need built, and he thrust deeper, harder and faster until finally she cried out with her climax, moving wildly on him. After he shuddered with his own release, she collapsed on him.

He stroked her gently, his fingers combing through her hair and continuing lower over her back, down over the curve of her bottom, playing lightly along the back of her thigh.

"That was rushed," he said, his voice husky. "Next time will be slow for you. I want to pleasure you for hours, to excite you, make you reach the most climaxes ever. I want my hands and my mouth all over you and I want you to touch and kiss me," he said, raising his head to kiss her shoulder.

She slid down beside him and he pulled her close into his embrace. "You're quiet, Vivian."

"I want you in my arms, Mike. At least for tonight. I'm not going to be in your bed every night and you're not going to be in mine."

"Shh. Stop worrying. This is just the first night. You can sleep in your room tomorrow night and I'll go back to the guesthouse if you want."

"No, just sleep in here without me."

"Fine. But tonight we're together and I want to hold you and to make love to you. You are so sexy, darlin'. You have no idea what you do to me," he whispered. "Stay here with me now. I want another night with you."

"How can I resist you, Mike?" She kissed him

passionately, rolling on top of him, and in minutes she felt his arousal again.

They made love once more and afterward, she fell asleep in his arms.

The next four nights she didn't see Mike at all. He ate with the men and he didn't come up to her house while she was downstairs. She missed him. The farewell party for Slade was going to be Thursday night and he would leave Friday for south Texas.

On Tuesday at about six, she heard a pickup and glanced out the window to see Mike heading toward the house. He had on working clothes, a cotton shirt, jeans, his gray hat and his boots, and he looked fantastic to her. She hurried to meet him.

"Hello," she said, opening the back door.

"Damn, I've missed you," he said, wrapping his arms around her and kissing her.

For a couple of seconds, she didn't know whether to tell him to slow down or to kiss him back. His lips took away her decision. Wrapping her arms around his neck, she clung to him and kissed him in return. The only thought she had left was how much she wanted him.

Finally, he leaned away, his gaze roaming over her. "You do look good enough to eat. Or something even more fun. Damn, I've missed you," he said again.

"I've missed you. What brings you here?"

"The party for Slade. What can I do for you? Do you want Henry and me to cook? I can barbeque."

"Fine. If you're half as good as Henry, we'll have a wonderful dinner."

"I'll get ribs and steaks—how's that?"

"Excellent." She gave him a brief rundown of the other party plans. "I think we're getting things lined up. How's it going on the ranch?"

"I'm trying to help Slade get ready to move when his sons come up and I'm busy trying to do my job, too. That's why you haven't seen me."

"I thought maybe you decided to stay in the guesthouse."

"No, I'm staying here. See, this place is so big you don't know who's here and who's not. I'm in my suite, but not until about ten or eleven at night. Want me to call you and you can come over tonight?" he asked with laughter in his voice.

"Thank you, but I'll pass at that hour. I may be sound asleep."

"I'll promise to get you back to sleep."

Laughing, she shook her head.

"I'll get back with you, darlin'. For now, I just wanted to see about the party. We're going to have a crowd. People in the next six counties know him and like him and want to say goodbye."

"I'm sure of that. Thane certainly loved him." She felt the sadness then. "It seems like he should be here, Mike."

He hugged her. "It seems like that to me as well, too, and often—but not because of the ranch. I didn't know him here."

"Out-of-the-blue it just hits me that Thane's gone

and he'll never be back. Sometimes it takes my breath away. Other times I can cope with it."

"It'll get easier with time, I guess."

"It already has a little. Part of that is because of you. You're full of life and you've filled a void." Turning to Mike to fill that void meant taking big risks that she would be hurt even more because Mike would never really fill the void. She didn't expect anything lasting with Mike. He was helping her get over Thane, but in doing so she was going to fall in love with him and be hurt again.

He gave her another hug and stepped away. "I have to go back, darlin'. Afraid I won't see you tonight unless you want me to just tiptoe in and slip into bed with you."

She smiled at him. "You might try and see what happens."

"Then I just might be back earlier this evening."

Seven

The party drew even more people than they had expected. But they had enough food because Henry and Mike had planned for hundreds. After all, Slade had worked at the Tumbling T for sixty years, first for Thane's grandfather and then Thane. He'd been just eighteen when he'd started working for the Warners.

It was three in the morning when the last guest finally left and Vivian lay in bed in Mike's arms.

"The party was a success, darlin'."

"Thanks for all you did. Slade and his family had a good time and that idea of presenting him with a stuffed Longhorn head to mount on the wall—that was a masterful touch, Mike. His little grandson's eyes were enormous. They loved those big horns.

The best part was that bull died of old age so it wasn't killed for its horns."

"Those horns will give the old man some memories and he can tell his friends some of the cattle stories."

"Another nice thing—neither Leon nor Clint Woodson was there."

"I noticed. I wondered about Woodson and I'm glad he stayed away. I guess you got your message across."

"I think you did. They think I'm your woman."

"At this point in life, I'd say they're right," he said, nuzzling her ear and sending chills down her spine.

She rolled over on top of him, looking down at him. Before she could say or do anything, he reached out and straddled her face in his hands.

"C'mere, my woman," he said, pulling her closer so he could kiss her.

She held him tightly, closing her eyes and kissing him in return.

It was daylight when they stopped.

They'd made love all night long, which was a good thing, she later reasoned, because all the next week— his first as the official Tumbling T foreman—she didn't see any sign of Mike. But she had a new worry looming in her life.

She had missed a period.

She didn't think she could possibly be pregnant because she and Thane had tried so many times and she hadn't gotten pregnant. Besides, she and Mike had always used protection. She couldn't imagine that was it, but to eliminate the possibility, she got a test kit.

It was the next day when she used it. She followed the directions then waited the allotted minutes. They seemed to be more like years as she anticipated the results. When the timer dinged, she looked down at the stick—unable to believe what she was seeing.

She laid it aside and immediately called her doctor to make an appointment to go to Dallas tomorrow.

She was pregnant with Mike's baby.

Stunned, she first felt a huge rush of joy. She was going to have a baby.

"Oh, Thane," she whispered. "Why couldn't it have been yours? A baby we both would have loved." A baby that might have kept him from going into the service.

Instead, she was going to have Mike's baby. She stiffened and sat up, blinking and turning cold. Mike was an alpha male through and through, and he would have all the coinciding typical attitudes toward an unexpected pregnancy and a baby. A baby born to an unwed mother. A baby born to a widowed mom. Mike would absolutely insist on marriage and it wouldn't make an iota of difference to him that love wasn't in his equation.

She didn't want to marry when he didn't love her. She loved him and he could be so much fun, but marriage needed love on both sides. Love was the stuff that got couples through when things were rough. Mike wasn't in this affair for love and her wealth might cause problems.

She put her head in her hands, trying to think of how to deal with him. She couldn't come up with any happy solution. Nor did she have anyone she could trust for advice—she wasn't that close to anyone. No one except Millie. She worked with Millie and they had a good relationship. Millie would be infinitely better than her mother that thought made her shake her head and laugh sarcastically. Her mother would be aghast and want to marry her off to the first possible candidate who would fit her mother's qualifications—good job, old money, right contacts, right country clubs. No, there was no hope there. She couldn't bear to be locked into a marriage without love on Mike's part. She'd marry him in a second if she believed he loved her, but she didn't think he would change and fall in love. If they married, he would worry about her inheritance for the rest of his life—unless she gave it to charity and lived on his income. If he didn't like it today, she felt certain he wouldn't like it tomorrow or the next year or the year after that. She'd give that fortune to charity if Mike would really love her, but she didn't think he was falling in love at all.

When and how was she going to tell him? She groaned and locked her fingers together. She didn't want to tell him because from that moment on, he would try to get her to marry him, probably until she gave in and did so. She'd better get her plans made because he would be taking charge as soon as she made the announcement.

That night she ate early and shut herself in her

room. She didn't want to encounter Mike until she had an agenda for herself and was ready to deal with him.

In fact, she didn't see him for the next week and she no longer was making an effort to avoid him. She didn't need to because he didn't come home early enough for them to see each other. She wondered if they were growing apart. Then she realized he had a lot more to do with Slade gone and after a time things would settle into a routine.

Late in the afternoon she was in her studio when she glanced outside, looking at the landscaped yard that took lots of money to maintain and keep watered. Maybe she should sell the ranch and move back to Dallas and then work out with Mike how they would deal with both of them having their child in their lives.

Tears started and she wiped her eyes. Crying wouldn't be good for her or for her baby. She heard a light knock on her open door and turned to see Henry.

"Come in, Henry."

He walked into the studio and strolled around, looking at the paintings she had lined up against the wall and on her easel. "You're a good artist, Vivian."

She set aside her brush, wiped her hands and sat in a nearby chair. "Sit down, Henry. I know you didn't come up here to look at my art. What's up?"

Sitting in a maroon leather chair, he turned to face her. "Millie will tell you our news today, too, but I wanted to talk to you myself. We're expecting our first child."

"Congratulations! That's wonderful. I'm sure you're both happy."

"Yes, we are," he said, grinning. "Millie feels good and the doc said everything is fine. I know you want your bodyguard nearby, so if this isn't going to work, we'll do something else, but we'd like to move out of this house into a house here on the ranch. We'll be happy still living here on the ranch, but we want our own house and our own yard."

She nodded. "I can understand that. Maybe we can get you an assistant who would stay in the house at night. What do you think?"

"I think that would be a good solution. In fact, I have a friend who I'd recommend for the job."

"Well, that was easy," she said smiling. She wished she could solve her problems as quickly.

Henry stood and walked toward the door, turning to face her. "I'll talk to my friend if you'd like and tell him if he is interested to call you."

"Thank you. That'd be good. And tell Millie to come in here when she's finished working on those expense sheets for me." She gave him a sincere grin. "I'm so happy for both of you. That's wonderful news."

"We think so," he said with a big smile and she felt a wistful pang, knowing Mike was not going to be so happy with her news. She had no idea how or when she would tell him.

She didn't see Millie for another hour until she

had put away her paints and was getting ready to go to the kitchen and eat an early dinner.

Millie knocked on the open door and came inside with papers in her hand. She was a willowy blonde and her pregnancy definitely didn't show.

"Millie, please close the door," Vivian said, standing and crossing the room. "Henry told me your news and I'm so happy for you. Congratulations," she said and hugged Millie lightly.

Millie smiled. "Thank you. We're so excited. We've wanted to have a baby and I had about given up and—surprise, we're going to have one! We're both thrilled. Henry is kind of silly about it, he's so excited."

"Sit down, please. That's wonderful. Be thankful you have Henry."

She laughed. "I've very thankful I have Henry." She glanced down at the papers in her hand, almost as if she just remembered them. "Here are your expense reports," she said, holding them out.

Vivian scanned them then put them on the table. "How are you feeling?"

"I feel great. I have a doctor in Dallas I like and when I'm in my last month, we'll probably move to the city. But we'll be back after the baby is born and my mom is coming to stay with us for a week."

"That's something you'll never hear me say. My mom would never come. She'd send someone. Partly because she can't imagine anyone taking care of a newborn unaided. I don't know what she thinks women do all over the world. Not everyone can hire a nurse or nanny," she said and they both laughed.

"Millie, I want to talk to you. We've been friends now for the past three years. I haven't told anyone this and I'm going to have to figure out how to deal with it, but...I'm pregnant."

Millie squealed and hugged Vivian. "Congratulations, yourself!

"Well, you're the only one who knows and you may tell Henry, but the dad doesn't know, so tell Henry to keep my news quiet."

"I won't tell another soul." She placed a hand over her heart as if swearing an oath. "Would you like one of my baby books? I have a bunch and I've already read a couple that I thought were good."

"Thanks, I would love to look at them." Vivian looked away a moment. "I hate to tell someone else first before I tell the father, but I don't think it's going to work out so well when I tell him."

"He doesn't like children?"

"Oh, no, that's not it. He doesn't like my money."

"Oh," she repeated.

I'm trying to get in mind what I want to do. I haven't known this long myself."

"Well, I hope you work it out and I'm sorry, because this should be the happiest time. Maybe your money will be more welcome now that there's a baby to spend it on. Henry would be turning cartwheels if I had a lot."

Vivian looked down at her diamond pendant. "Thane and I tried to have a baby. If only it had worked out then, but it didn't," she said. "Ah, well. Bring the baby books when it's convenient. If I'm not here, you can just put them on my desk in the study. No one ever goes in there except to clean. Thane and I were the only ones who used that room."

"I will. I hope you work things out. I'm glad we're having babies at the same time. Our kids can be friends."

Vivian smiled and nodded, going to open the door to see Millie out. She sighed and turned away. She had a lot of decisions to make. It was May now and Slade was gone. If she left the ranch, she would have to put it up for sale and that would hurt a lot of people, but there seemed little point in her staying. Eventually, she would have to leave it and get closer to a private school in Dallas, probably choosing the private schools she attended. The biggest decision she faced right now was when she would tell Mike. But she needed to have a plan in place before he started trying to take charge. For the ranch, Thane had picked one of the best foremen to run the business from what Thane and Slade had said about Mike. As far as meddling in her life, that was a whole different story.

She decided to forego dinner and stay in her suite, working on her life plan. By nightfall, she wasn't any closer to an agenda and later she lay in bed in the dark, thinking about what she wanted to do. She placed her hand on her stomach. Her baby and Mike's. Tears came and she wiped them away. This should be one of the happiest times in her life and here she was, crying. She had to stop thinking about that and just make plans. If nothing else, she'd move back to Dallas, buy a house, get a nursery ready and hire a nanny.

She thought about Millie's mother coming and smiled. Her mother had immediately turned each of her own children over to nannies. Vivian wanted some help, but she wasn't giving up taking care of her precious little baby that she had wanted so badly when Thane was alive.

She would ask Mike if he would mind if they named a boy Thane. She would like that and maybe Mike would, too. Hopefully, it would be one thing they could agree on. She might as well break the news to him soon and let him start adjusting. Was the fight just beginning or could they work it out peacefully? Mike had his moments when he surprised her and was incredibly kind and considerate—like the night when she felt so despondent telling him goodnight and he had turned around to look at her and then came back to hold her and kiss away her tears.

She didn't expect that kind of reaction this time, but she could always hope. There was just no way to accurately guess his reaction to learning he was about to be a dad.

Mike worked until late every day and he got up early in the morning to eat and get to work. Slade had made everything look so damned easy. Or had a lot of things happened after Slade left and it was just pure coincidence that he seemed to have way more to do than Slade had?

It was Thursday and Mike hadn't seen Vivian in days and he missed her. He wanted to take her out the soonest possible weekend he felt he could get away. They needed a night to themselves. He needed a night with her. What he wanted was a weekend with her where they could get away from the ranch and its problems and just enjoy each other's company and spend hours making love.

He made a mental note to find her tonight and ask her to spend the weekend with him.

He had three guys who were great cowboys. He'd be able to fall back on any one of them if something came up and he was away from the ranch or unable to work for any reason. Slade had told him to find three and Mike had taken his advice. It was a good feeling knowing these men were there. It was also a good feeling knowing Leon was gone. He hadn't worked but a short time with the man, so losing Leon wasn't a blow as far as Mike was concerned and he didn't have to worry about Leon and Vivian. He didn't have to worry about Clint and Vivian either and that was good. The neighboring rancher hadn't been around in a while.

Thinking of Vivian made him yearn to hear the sound of her voice. He tried calling her but the phone rang unanswered until her voice mail came on. It had been like that for days. He ended up not leaving a message when he got another call. He took it and got caught up in discussing some missing cattle. He turned his pickup around and headed in the opposite direction and forgot about talking to Vivian.

It was evening when he got back to the house. He had seen lights on in her suite when he had driven up, so he walked upstairs and knocked. She opened the door.

She was in cutoffs and a blue T-shirt but to him she looked beautiful. "Hi, stranger," he said.

"Hi. You're working late now and a lot more."

"I sure am. I didn't realize how much Slade did. He made it look easy. I don't have the knack for making it look easy or be easy. Can I come in for a minute?"

"Sure," she said, stepping back. He walked in to stand close to her.

"You look wonderful."

"Thank you, Mike. We haven't seen each other much."

"No, and I want to change that. Let me take you to Dallas tomorrow night. Some place fun or even just to your condo. I want to get away from the ranch and the problems here. We can go to dinner and then you pick it—dancing, a show. What would you like to do? Anything sounds good to me."

"That would be fine. Let's go to dinner at the club in downtown Dallas. It's quiet and has a piano player and excellent food by a super chef. We can stay in my condo again."

"Oh, baby, you have a date. I can't wait to go."

"Are you sorry you have Slade's job?"

"Not at all. It's just that a lot has happened this

past week. It'll settle down. On top of other problems, we need rain and a lot of it. I'm sure we'll eventually get it. Vivian, do you know where your phone is?"

"Yes. It's in the other room on my desk."

"For a couple days now I haven't been able to get you when I call."

"I'll pay more attention. I was probably wrapped up in painting or something and didn't even hear it. I didn't think you would call me when you're working."

"Well, I have and I'd like to get you when I call. Is anything wrong?"

"Wrong? No," she said and smiled at him.

"You seem preoccupied," he said, feeling an invisible wall between them that he didn't expect. He couldn't figure out why he felt that way when he never had before with her. He wanted to take her in his arms, kiss her for the next hour and make love to her all night, but he had a feeling if he tried to hug her, she would stop him. They stood looking at each other and his suspicions grew that something was wrong, but he didn't know what and she obviously wasn't going to tell him.

He closed the gap between them, seeing her eyes widen and a flush make her cheeks pink. He wrapped his arms around her, leaned over her and kissed her. For a moment she didn't respond, didn't do anything, but then her arms went around his neck and her lips yielded to his.

When she kissed him in return, she was as passionate and sexy as ever. Shaking, he wanted her with all his being. He tightened one arm around her while he ran his other hand over her, tugging her shirt out of her shorts and slipping beneath it to caress her breast.

His heart pounded and he regretted that he had waited this long to come see her. He stepped back a moment and, watching her, yanked her T-shirt over her head to toss it away. Her bra was gone swiftly and then he unfastened her shorts and let them fall around her ankles and she stepped out of them.

He looked at her, his gaze drifting slowly over her as if he had to memorize every inch. He finally looked into her eyes again and saw longing and desire in her gaze. Wrapping his arms around her, he kissed her hard again.

"I've missed you, called you a dozen damn times, wanted to see you, but every night I got in too late to bother you," he whispered as he showered kisses on her, leaning down to run his tongue over her nipple, his hands sliding over her. "You feel wonderful. I want to spend the weekend in bed with you." He leaned back as she opened her eyes to look at him.

"I'll take you out first and feed you," he said, "and we can dance a few dances if you want. I need you, Vivian."

She looked up at him. "I don't think you really need me. You can be so wonderful, Mike."

He focused more intently on her. "I'm waiting for the other half of that sentence," he said, feeling anxious, more certain than ever that something was wrong between them. He thought of all the unanswered phone calls. "Vivian—"

She slipped her hand to his nape and brought his head down to kiss him. One touch was all it took. He picked her up to carry her to bed and he forgot his worries.

The next day, Mike tried to slip out of bed without waking her, but she opened her eyes and turned to him. He came back to take her into his arms and kiss her and it was a little more than an hour later that he got out of bed again.

"This time I'm going. I need to go to work, but I don't want to leave you. I'll see you tonight about seven. I'll make the reservations—"

She smiled. "I will. I'm the club member." Her gaze ran over him and she rolled over to get closer to him and run her hand across his chest. "You are one sexy man."

"I'm glad you think so." He kissed her. "Oh, hell, I can be late to work once." He threw himself onto the bed.

Minutes later, after some serious kissing, she pushed him away.

"Go on. We'll kiss tonight."

He looked into her gorgeous blue eyes. "Vivian, you're beautiful."

"Thank you. You need to move, Mike." She scooted across the bed and bent to grab her T-shirt from the floor, glancing over her shoulder at him.

He straightened his clothes and crossed the room.

"If I walk down the hall to my suite, am I going to encounter anyone?"

"No, usually they clean this floor on Tuesdays."

"Usually. That leaves a loophole. See you tonight." He left, hurrying down the hall and already thinking about the evening. He intended to ask her about the missed phone calls. She needed to take his calls or tell him why she hadn't answered and whether it had been deliberate because she hadn't wanted to talk to him. But why would that be? When they had made love, it was as if everything was fine between them and the uneasy feeling he'd had for a few minutes had vanished into the night and never returned. But not taking his calls was odd. He had a feeling there was something he was missing. If so, surely he would find out what it was tonight.

Vivian finished dressing almost an hour before she expected to see Mike. He had called three times today. First he called to check on the reservations, the second time just to talk to her and the third time to tell her he would try to be on time. If she hadn't been facing the evening that she knew was ahead, she would have laughed at his last call, but she couldn't. She had the feeling that tonight would change their relationship forever and she didn't think that the change would be good.

She was going to tell him about the baby.

At seven o'clock she checked herself again in front of a full-length mirror and turned first one way and then another. She looked at herself and ran her hand over her flat stomach. She wore a slim, sleeveless, figure-clinging black dinner dress that ended at her knees. It had a deep V-neckline and the diamond pendant was perfect with it. She did not look pregnant at all, but then it was so early.

Her phone buzzed and she answered to hear Mike's greeting. Her pulse sped up at the sound of his voice and she wondered how long she would continue to have such an intense reaction to just seeing him or hearing him speak.

"Hi. I'm downstairs and I'm ready. Shall I come up or do you want to come down?"

"I'll be right down. I'm ready."

"Wow, you really are a wonderful woman— beautiful and on time," he teased. "See you in the hall."

He was gone before she could say goodbye. "If you only knew. You're not going to feel that way about me later tonight. And I won't feel the same about you, either," she said.

She glanced at a picture of her with Thane on their wedding day. A sharp pain stabbed her. She had been so happy at that moment when that picture was taken. The future looked golden, perfect with Thane in it.

She picked up the picture. "How I wish I could have given this news of a baby to you. You would have been the happiest man on the planet. Well, maybe you and Henry would have been. It didn't work out that way. I love you. I miss you so much." She thought of the man waiting downstairs for her.

"In so many ways, he's a good guy. But I guess I don't have to tell you that."

She replaced the picture, gathered her things and left her suite. Mike stood at the bottom of the stairs and watched her as she walked down. As usual, at the sight of him, her heart beat faster. She wanted to laugh and dance and go to her condo and make love later. She didn't know at what point tonight she would break the news to him. Or should she wait until the next weekend? It wouldn't change anything, she rationalized. She sighed, knowing in her heart she should tell him tonight so they could both get on with the changes in their lives.

"Hi, handsome cowboy," she said, looking at him.

"You know, taking you out for a fun night and a good dinner and going to your condo afterward seemed a great idea at the time. But right at this moment, looking at you as you came down the stairs, I want to carry you right back upstairs and take that sexy black dress off you and kiss you all over, put my hands all over you and make love to you the rest of the night."

Dropping the little purse she carried, she wrapped her arms around his neck. She stood on the second step that put her on his level and she could look directly into his eyes. "I won't argue with that one," she said, wanting him with all her being and wondering if this would be the last time they would make love. She had a feeling he wasn't going to take her news well at all.

His eyes narrowed. "Do you really mean that?

I can call and cancel our reservations. I don't want you to get a bad name with your club."

"I won't. This is kind of fun, being on your level."

"I don't care where you stand, you're irresistible," he said, nuzzling her neck and then kissing her.

After a moment, she placed her hand against him and leaned back slightly. "Call the club. I can go get you a beer or a drink or whatever you want."

"I want you. Put some steaks out to thaw. By breakfast, they may be ready to cook."

"I've already put steaks out. I had a feeling we might not ever get out of the house when the time arrived."

"I promise you, I will take you out, just not to-night."

"I think this is better." She dropped a light kiss on his mouth. "I'll go get our drinks and you call the club and cancel the reservations."

"Sounds like a plan," he said.

She went to the kitchen and got a beer and a glass of water for herself and carried them to the family room. It was her favorite room because it was informal, a colorful, cheerful space that she enjoyed.

He caught up with her to take the drinks from her hands and set them on a game table. He shed his charcoal sports jacket and turned to reach for her. "Come here, Vivian. I just can't wait."

"Mike, you're going to have to wait a little. I want to talk first. We have something to talk about."

He looked intently at her.

"Okay, we'll talk," he said. "But first I'll have that beer. This sound serious."

"It is serious," she said, knowing there was no going back now as she looked into his curious green eyes.

Mike took a swallow of his beer. He wondered if she had decided to sell the ranch. He couldn't figure out why she stayed now. If she did sell it, he wouldn't care. All along, he'd planned to leave when his three months were up, but that had been before they had slept together. Since that time, he did some rethinking on that and decided he would stay where he was, at least as long as Vivian was in his life. Continuing their affair sounded good to him.

He took another pull on the beer bottle then set it down and looked at her. "What do we need to discuss?"

"I don't know any way to say it except just to come right out and say it. I was shocked and you're going to be shocked, too."

He figured he knew what she was about to say and said it for her. "You're going to sell the ranch and move back to Dallas."

To his surprise, she shook her head. "No, not at this time. I may do that in the not-too-distant future, though. No, I have something else to tell you. Mike, I'm pregnant."

Her words hit him like a lightning bolt. He felt stunned, paralyzed, as if the breath had been knocked out of him. He stared at her and repeated the words, as if doing so would help him process them. "You're pregnant."

"Yes, I am. I bought a pregnancy test kit and then I went to see a doctor. I'm definitely pregnant."

Once more he felt as if he were back in a mine-field in Afghanistan. He stood, picked up his beer and walked to the window, just to move around and take a moment to think. She waited in silence and he was thankful for the moment to try to wrap his thoughts around her news. Finally, he turned around to face her.

"I don't know how shocked you were, but this is not anything I anticipated. I'm going to be a dad. Vivian. That is something I absolutely never expected."

She sat in a wing chair and sipped her water, waiting quietly, saying nothing, giving him the time he needed to work through the announcement.

"I thought you said you'd had trouble getting pregnant. And we used a condom, always."

"Right and right. Thane and I wanted a baby, but it just never happened." She set down her glass and looked up at him. "Mike, I'm financially taken care of. I don't need anything, so you're really off the hook, so to speak."

He took a long drink of beer, more to give himself some time to absorb the news of his change in status than for thirst. He had gotten Vivian pregnant and he was going to be a dad. That had seemed impossible with the protection they had used and the fact that she and Thane had wanted and tried for a baby but she'd never gotten pregnant.

"If you had told me to guess what you were going to tell me, we would have been here until the sun was high tomorrow and I still wouldn't have come up with the correct answer. Pregnancy is the last possibility I thought might happen."

"I agree. I felt just as shocked as you must feel because Thane and I wanted a baby so badly. When everything physically checked out as normal, the doctor said I might have been too uptight about it and if I could just relax I might get pregnant. I must have been relaxed with you."

He couldn't begin to label the emotions that were running through him. All he could do was state the obvious. "Wow. This is a big one. Our lives will change forever."

"That's right. Other than you and Millie and Henry and my doctor, no one knows. I would just as soon keep it that way for a little while until we sort out how we'll deal with the future."

"I agree with that one. I want to be able to answer questions." Then her words finally found their way into his brain. "Millie and Henry? You've told them?"

"I guess Henry hasn't said anything to you yet. Millie is pregnant and not much farther along than I am. I told them I hadn't told you yet. They're not going to say anything about it."

He looked at her. She had turned her head away and was sitting quietly again, giving him more time to think. A baby... Financially, she wouldn't ever need anything from him, but there was more to raising a baby than money. He thought of his own family, his mother.

He knew what he had to do. Just as he had been raised to believe the man should have the money and be the provider, he also had been raised to believe in shouldering his responsibilities and that if possible, children should have their mother and dad. His mother and dad had instilled strong beliefs in their kids and he didn't see any choice about it.

He went to her side and squatted down next to her, resting his hands on her forearms. "Vivian, I want to know my baby. I want to watch my child grow up. It seems to me, there's an obvious solution. Vivian, will you marry me?"

Eight

Vivian stood up and took a step back as she shook her head. "That's a knee-jerk reaction and no, I will not marry you. Your mom raised four kids by herself. I am financially very well-fixed and I can hire all the help I need and build the kind of house I want and do what I want."

This wasn't the reaction to his proposal that Mike was hoping for. He closed the distance between them. "Are you thinking about this baby at all?"

"Definitely," she replied. "You're doing exactly what I expected you to do. I knew you'd propose to me tonight."

"And that's so terrible? You don't want a dad for your baby?"

"You're our baby's dad, but I don't want to marry

you. You're proposing to me only because I'm pregnant."

"Well, hell yes, I am."

"When I marry again, I want the man who proposes to me to love me. Really love me," she said softly.

He stared at her a moment. "Vivian—"

"Don't say you love me when you don't. You have never declared your love."

"And you haven't said you love me. That doesn't mean we can't fall in love."

"Mike," she said quietly, "when we fall in love and then you ask me if I'll marry you, I'll say yes."

"You're being ridiculous about this," he said, trying to hang on to his temper.

"No, I'm not. Now I'm the old-fashioned one who wants to get married because a guy is in love with me. You're not. If we fall in love later, we can talk about marrying then. Life is tough. Marriages don't work well where there's no love. Love can get you through a lot."

He ran a hand through his hair and blew out a breath, his patience fraying. "I live down the hall from you. We're living in the same damn house and we're in the same damn bed a lot of nights. That's mighty close to being married. If we get married and live the same way we do now, we can raise our baby, fall in love, have more kids, live like normal parents—"

She held up a palm, interrupting his argument.

"Are you going to be happy married to me with all my money?"

He stared at her and it was difficult to get his breath. Her logic was skewed as far as he was concerned, but she was right. Her damn money was a problem. He didn't like it now and he wouldn't like it tomorrow and he hadn't liked it since he first drove up to the ranch to see about working for her.

"No, I won't be happy if you want an honest answer. That is an old-fashioned view. I'm trying to get beyond it and be happy about it like some other guys would be. I can adjust, I think, to having a very wealthy wife. I want my baby in my life. I want you in my life. I—"

She closed the space between them to put her finger on his lips. "Shh. Don't you say you love me, because you don't."

Anger blazed in his expression and they stared at each other. Suddenly, he wrapped his arms around her, drew her against him and kissed her hard and passionately, leaning over her until she wrapped her arms around him and kissed him in return. His kiss was demanding, thorough, sexy, his lips challenging her to do what his words could not. Forget everything else but the passion between them.

As he held her, his mouth hard on hers, Vivian's anger boiled because she loved him and she knew she did. She had fallen in love while he hadn't and that hurt. He wanted sex. She wanted love and sex. She kissed him, feeling as if she really kissed him goodbye. They would never have the same relationship they'd had before tonight and the news of the baby.

His hand slipped beneath the deep vee of her dress and his fingers stroked her breast through her lacy bra. Desire burned away her anger and she wanted him. She stopped thinking about the future and being pregnant. Instead, she thought about the here and now. Right now, she wanted Mike to make love to her. She wanted to lose herself in hot sex and stop fighting and quit worrying about tomorrow and next month and nine months from now.

He must have wanted the same thing because he picked her up and carried her to a downstairs bedroom. He shoved the door closed and in minutes they were both naked. He picked her up to place her on the bed and then he moved over her, between her legs, coming down to enter her in one smooth motion.

Crying out in passion, she wrapped her legs around him and arched against him. While he thrust into her, she ran her hands over his back and his butt, tugging him against her as she thrashed beneath him. Finally, she arched her back and let her climax burst through her. Almost at the same time, he shuddered with his own release.

Minutes later they were still gasping for breath. He kept her with him as he rolled over and held her. "Vivian, marry me. It'll be good and we'll fall in love."

His voice was deep in the quiet room and she hurt. She was tempted to say yes, but all she had to do was think about what it would be like if she married

Mike. They would go through the motions and everyone would congratulate them, but they wouldn't have that wonderful happiness that two people in love had.

She cupped his jaw with her hand so he would pay attention to her. "Mike, I've been married to a man I loved with all my heart. I know how good it can be. I know how exciting it can be. I would be miserable if we married now. You wouldn't be happy. In bed and having sex—yes, you'd like that and so would I, but there's a lot of living beyond that and love is important."

He stroked her hair and held her close. "You're probably right about love, Vivian. I think I'm probably right, too. I think we'd fall in love if you'd give us a chance."

"I'm going back to Dallas for a while to think about what I want to do. I want some time and some space."

"This is why you haven't taken my calls."

She wouldn't lie to him. "Yes, it is."

"I should have known there was something."

"You've been busy and you have a new job."

He hesitated a second, his eyes skirting from hers. "Do you know which one of the guys Lewis Owens is?"

"Yes, I do. Thane liked Lewis and said he worked hard."

He looked back at her. "I want him next in line after me. If I'm gone, I'm turning things over to Lewis."

"When your three months are up that you promised Thane, you'll be gone, won't you?" He'd already been there more than a month so he had less than two months left now.

"I promise I won't leave you in the lurch."

She felt the loss times two. Mike would be gone from her life and from the ranch.

Before he left, there was something she had to ask him. "I want to ask you—if we have a little boy, will it be all right with you to name him Thane?"

"That's fine with me."

"You know I don't even know your full name."

"Michael Cassano Moretti. A little Italian influence there, I think. Don't hang those on a little baby, but then you won't be using any of my names. I'm sure if it's a boy you'll name him Thane Warner—right?" he asked.

"I don't know, Mike. We have time to think about names."

He sat up on the side of the bed. "I'll go shower and cook those steaks if you want."

"I can probably find something Francie left that would be a lot easier to just heat and eat "

"I'd like that. I'll probably be hungry later. I'm not right now." He left to go into the adjoining bathroom.

As soon as he closed the door, she got out of bed and gathered her clothes to take them to her room and shower.

When she went downstairs later, there was no sign of Mike. In the kitchen she found a note in neat handwriting: *I need to think things over. I will talk to you tomorrow.*

She wondered if he would talk to her tomorrow or if that was just putting off saying goodbye. She decided to pack her things that she wanted for the next week and go to Dallas to stay in her condo. She could get away from Mike, from hurtful memories, from ranch responsibilities. She'd leave a note for Francie and give her the week off. Mike ate his meals with the men anyway.

Tears fell. She would miss Mike. She had done what she knew she shouldn't—she had fallen in love with him and it hurt to decline his proposal, but she didn't want to marry him when he wasn't in love and he still couldn't cope with her inheritance at all.

Why was he so wonderful in so many other ways, but not in that way? So old-fashioned and unyielding. He wanted to marry her anyway, but she couldn't see how marriage without love on his part would ever work out.

If they married without his love, it would be like tonight—he would just leave as he had done now. She couldn't see him anymore because there wasn't any future in it. They couldn't continue this relationship. She wasn't going to just be there for sex and no love.

She sank into a chair, put her head in her hands and cried. She missed Mike already. If only he felt differently…

Her hand rested on her middle as if cradling the baby that grew there. "Michael Thane Warner," she whispered aloud. "Thane Michael Warner." She didn't care if she had a boy or a girl. She just wanted a healthy baby. "I love both of you," she said. Thane was gone but he'd never had a choice. But Mike did. He'd made his choice. He wasn't in love and he had let her go.

Tomorrow, she was leaving the ranch and she didn't think she would ever come back to live there.

Mike showered and dressed for work, hoping he could keep his mind on what he was doing long enough to be useful. He was going to be a dad. Vivian was carrying his baby. What a muddle he had made of things. She wanted love. She should get a little more practical and think about having a dad around for their baby. He expected her to sell the ranch. There was nothing to hold her here. He had planned to leave. The worst would be putting the ranch on the market and having Clint Woodson buy it. Mike shook his head. He wasn't going to worry over that one. He had enough to think about.

Since Vivian was financially covered, the dynamics were different than they would have been otherwise. She didn't need Mike to help support their baby. She didn't need him at all. She was independent in every way.

He would just have to let her go and they would have to work out some kind of schedule where they could each spend time with their child. This was something he had never expected to have happen in his life. He dreaded going home and telling his mother. She would never understand why he and Vivian weren't married.

As soon as he was dressed for the day, he went downstairs. Vivian was nowhere around, not that he expected to see her. He thought about the unanswered phone calls. She had been avoiding him. He'd had a slight nagging feeling that something was wrong, but he'd shrugged it off. Now he knew he had been right to feel that way.

In a couple of months, his life would be changing again. He had planned to leave when the three months were up anyway. This wasn't the place for him to work. He had always felt there was no future for him with Vivian. Not when she had "billion-dollar heiress" attached to her résumé.

"Damn," he said softly as he moved around the kitchen, pouring orange juice, getting black coffee, making toast. If he stayed, they might fall in love. If he left, they for sure wouldn't. Falling in love would be best for their child, but could he live with her with all that money? Some men would think he was ridiculous and out of touch with this century, but he just wasn't wired to accept his wife having one of the biggest fortunes in the state.

Would Vivian be happy staying on the ranch? During the baby and toddler years, it would probably be better if he stayed on the ranch with her if she did. He still wanted to leave, but he couldn't walk away now. He needed to be here for Vivian and for his child. Then a thought struck him and he shook his head. Vivian might prefer that he get out of her life. She could date other men, meet someone else and get married.

That thought hurt. He didn't like to think of her out with any other man. He definitely didn't like to think about her marrying someone else and another man raising his child.

Mike swore again softly, raking his fingers through his hair and standing. His appetite was gone. He threw away the toast, put the dishes in the dishwasher and finally got his hat and left the house. He wouldn't come back until late. That was one thing he could lose himself in—hard, physical labor—and he welcomed it so he could stop thinking about Vivian.

He thought about moving back to the guesthouse. There was no point in it. He could stay right where he was in the main house and never see Vivian if she didn't want to see him or if he didn't want to see her. All suites on the second floor had outside exits. He would stay in the main house. He would do something to acknowledge Lewis taking more responsibility. If Lewis would accept moving up, Mike could let him move into the foreman's house and get it done over the way Lewis wanted.

And if Mike changed his mind about staying on the ranch, there was always the guesthouse that he could move back into.

He couldn't stop being amazed at the fact that he was going to be a dad. How long would it take for the shock to wear off? He wondered if Vivian would cooperate. She had sounded hurt, angry and matter-of-fact about the situation. Part of her easy acceptance was the security of the money, he was sure. That would take a number of worries away.

And it really left him free because she didn't want any monetary help from him and she didn't want to marry him. He could turn his back and walk away and she would merely say goodbye.

They weren't in love and that was another big factor. If they had been in love, the simple and instant solution would have been to get married.

That wasn't the case and it was one more reason for him to leave the Tumbling T Ranch. Although, he thought Vivian might be gone before he was.

He had a feeling that he and Vivian had spent their last night together. He didn't expect to see much of her from now on, though eventually, she would have to sit down with him and talk about their future and their baby.

He left the house and jumped into his pickup, hoping a day of work could take his mind off Vivian and the baby. He'd much prefer worrying about the ranch and a bunch of cattle.

It took all morning for Vivian to pack, and in the early afternoon, Henry carried her things to the limo. There were no calls from Mike and she knew they were over. They wouldn't ever keep that date to go to the club to dinner and go dancing. She missed him already and she hurt because she loved him. For the second time in her life she had fallen in love and it had come to a disastrous end. This time, though, it wasn't fate that had taken her man; it was her fortune.

"Stubborn, stubborn old-fashioned man," she

whispered. And he wouldn't change. It was ingrained in him.

She glanced around the suite, making sure one last time that she had everything then went downstairs. She wanted off the ranch, away from the memories with Mike. She had clung to the ranch and the memories she'd had there with Thane because they had been wonderful and a comfort. The memories of the happy times there with Mike just made her long for him and wish things were different when they never would be.

She hoped she could move back to the city, pick up her city life and her friends again and find someone to enjoy going out with, to have a casual, happy relationship with.

Henry approached her, insisting on carrying out the small tote bag she held. She was so grateful for him. He and Millie would be staying in one of Vivian's family's condos as long as she was in Dallas. It was close by and she could get him on his cell phone any time she needed him.

She was just about to leave when Millie appeared. "I put the baby books in the desk drawer in the library."

"Thank you. I already have them packed and in the car. Henry won't let me carry anything."

Millie laughed. "I'm sure he won't. I'm rather enjoying getting waited on hand and foot. Henry and I will be moving into the Dallas condo this afternoon so we'll be nearby. I'm getting things together now."

"I hope this isn't a big upheaval."

"Actually, we'll both be happy to be in Dallas. Henry isn't a cowboy and I love the city, so it will be a nice change."

"I'm glad." She gave Millie a few final instructions about her artwork then felt compelled to fill her in on her personal situation. "I've told Mike about the baby. He was shocked and he's probably still in shock, which I can understand."

Millie's expression sobered. "I hope you two can work things out. Henry says Mike is a really good guy like Thane was."

"Yes, he is. He asked me to marry him, but he's not in love and I don't think it would really work out."

"You don't think you would fall in love with each other?"

"I don't know, but for now that doesn't seem the thing to do."

"I hope you can work it out. I'm just so excited about us having babies around the same time."

Millie was due in December and Vivian in February. Their babies would grow up together. That was one thing Vivian could look forward to.

Millie said goodbye, going upstairs to get more things packed, and Vivian decided she needed one last look around the house before she got in the limo. She had put one of the baby books in her purse to read on the drive to Dallas. She really didn't know much about babies, but she was going to learn. She suspected she would learn very quickly.

She turned around as Mike came down the hall from the back.

"What are you doing here?" she asked.

"I heard you were ready to leave soon, so I thought I'd come say goodbye."

"Henry is loading the limo and it's waiting for me now."

"That's good." Mike walked up to her and touched her hand, rubbing it lightly with his fingers. She had the usual tingles that she got when she first saw him. That hadn't changed at all. And the sizzle increased when he held her hand firmly in his. She wanted his arms around her, his mouth on hers. She wanted to be with him, to have him hold and love her and tell her that he loved her, but that wasn't going to happen.

Saying goodbye now was going to be rough. In some ways, she wished he hadn't come back to say goodbye. She had been doing all right about leaving, but now it wasn't going to be easy to smile through telling him goodbye, knowing that it might be absolute.

Henry came in. "Hi, Mike. I didn't mean to interrupt anything." He turned to Vivian. "We have the car packed. Ben is ready to drive. Is there anything else?"

She shook her head.

"Then I think you should be ready to go in a couple of minutes."

"I'm in no hurry, Henry."

"Sure," he said and disappeared down the hall.

She turned back to Mike. "I guess this is good-bye for now."

He still ran his finger back and forth on her hand. "You'll be at your condo?"

"Yes, and you know my phone number." There was a moment of silence between them as their gazes locked, and Vivian felt the pain so sharply. She didn't want to think about how final in so many ways this goodbye would be.

He took her arm lightly. "Come here," he said and they walked into the library and he closed the door. He turned to look at her and his eyes looked dark and stormy. He slipped his arms around her waist and drew her to him to kiss her, his mouth covering hers and his tongue stroking hers.

She wanted his lovemaking. She wanted his strong body against hers and his strong arms around her while they kissed. She wanted his love. She wanted him in her life.

She knew that wasn't going to happen, but his body was hard and he was aroused, ready to love. She trembled and clung to him, kissing him with all the passion and need she could pour into their kiss.

She wanted to hold him, to hear words of love, to stay on the ranch with him. Instead, there were just the sounds of their heavy breathing as she shifted against him.

Finally, she leaned away a fraction. She wanted to say, "I love you," but she wasn't going to when he didn't love her. "I'd better get going."

Neither could she say goodbye. Because of their

baby, they had locked their lives together for the next twenty years or more, but this was goodbye to their nights of loving, goodbye to the hot sex and the fun, goodbye to the intimacy. Goodbye to spending time with him. She had to stop thinking about it or she would burst in to tears and she was not going to do that when she was with him. He had made his choice and was doing what he wanted to do. She just had to let him go.

Mike spoke in to the silence, erasing the need for her to utter the dreaded word. "Okay, Vivian. We'll talk. I'll call you and we can go out like we started to do."

"Sure, Mike," she said, knowing he wouldn't call and they wouldn't go out. This was goodbye.

He gave her a long look and then turned and left without looking back. She heard his boots as he went down the hall. She walked out, but he had already gone out of sight. She ran back into the library and closed the door, letting the tears fall.

When she got her emotions under control, she wiped her eyes and walked to the window to look out, knowing Mike had left and he probably wouldn't give a lot of thought to the past.

When would losing Mike stop hurting? Every place they had been together would stir memories and cause her pain if she was there again. How long would it be before it stopped aching to remember being with Mike? Was it going to hurt like this each time they had to get together after their baby was born?

The pain racked her, and she couldn't help wondering: Did he even hurt at all or wish things were different?

Nine

A week later as evening approached, Mike climbed into his pickup and turned to drive home. Home. He shook his head. He was beginning to think of the suite where he lived in the main house as his home. In reality, it was a temporary place that he really should move out of. He had moved in for Vivian, to help get rid of Clint. He must have succeeded because he hadn't heard a thing from her about Clint. Actually, he hadn't heard anything from her at all. Not since she'd left the ranch.

He missed her. The big house was empty without her. He worked late and he ate dinner with the men so that by the time he got to his suite he was pretty much ready for bed. Even then, he was still unable to sleep, even when he was exhausted.

He missed Vivian badly. He thought with extra work, hard work, he would drive away the loneliness and longing for her. Every time he reached for his phone to call her, he thought about the fortune she had, her net worth, her feelings about money and his views that she definitely found antiquated, and he decided against the call.

He couldn't change and she couldn't, either. He also didn't think she was in love with him. And he wasn't with her.

If you're not in love, why do you miss her so badly? asked an inner voice.

Because they'd had something good between them and they'd had fun together. He'd been in the military and she had been widowed, and when they met, both of them were ready for friends, a social life, a real life and getting out again, so they just clicked.

That answer had to suffice. Because he wasn't in love.

But when another week rolled past, Mike was still having a hard time forgetting her. He strolled through the mansion library, glancing at the books, but nothing grabbed his interest. And no one was around to talk to. Aside from Henry and Millie, the staff was still there, but he never saw them. They attended to the household chores when he was out on the ranch, except for Francie who didn't need to come down to cook for him at all.

And everywhere he looked he thought of Vivian.

He left the library and wandered up to his suite, telling himself he had other things to think about and some decisions to make. He thought about turning in his resignation. But if he got a job far away from Dallas or the Tumbling T, the places where Vivian would be, it would be more difficult working out how to get their baby back-and-forth.

If Vivian put the ranch on the market and Clint bought it, Mike wasn't staying and he didn't think a lot of the guys would stay. But if she sold the ranch, she wouldn't have much say about who bought it and she couldn't refuse to sell to Clint.

Mike swore and walked out on to his balcony. There was a starry sky overhead and a bright moon lighting the night. He missed her and he wanted her. Did that mean he was in love with her? He no longer knew the answer to that question. All he knew was that he couldn't deal with her fortune and he didn't want to.

He looked at the date on his watch. Mid-June. He had hoped as time passed that he would miss Vivian less, but he missed her more now than ever.

How had she come to be so important to him?

A couple of days ago he hadn't been able to resist the temptation and he'd called her to see how she was and to just hear her voice.

She'd said she felt fine, with no morning sickness. Her voice sounded guarded and they'd talked only briefly when she said she had to go. Since then he'd tried to call her a couple other times, but she never answered so he stopped trying.

How were they going to work out sharing a baby? He would have to see Vivian when he would pick up their baby, unless she hired someone to be there for that. The more he thought about it, the more certain he was that that was exactly what she'd do. And, most likely, she would marry again. That thought brought him up short and he cut it off. Another man with Vivian. Another man raising his child. Mike swore quietly. The image was too upsetting to contemplate.

He thought about going to bed, but he had slept with Vivian often enough that he missed her being with him. He pulled out his phone to call her then stared at it as he thought about all the reasons that was a bad move. She lived in Dallas now in that ritzy penthouse apartment. She might even be dating.

As he held the phone it buzzed with a new text. He dared to hope it would be Vivian. To his surprise it was from his army buddy Noah Grant.

Will be out of Rangers next month. Need to get together. Jake still over there. See you when I get home. Hope you like your job. How's Thane's wife? Lunch or dinner? I'll let you know when I'll be in area.

Mike smiled as he typed in a reply. In July, Noah would be home. Then Jake would be back last. If only Thane had made it and he had come home to the Tumbling T. Instead, Thane's wife was going to have Mike's baby. Not what Thane had intended when he'd sent Mike to the ranch. And she was leaving the ranch. Again, not what Thane had intended. Mike shook his head. Things hadn't gone well and he felt responsible for them being so far off course.

There were some pluses, though: Slade got to retire. Clint Woodson had stopped bothering Vivian; Lewis Owens was getting a well-deserved promotion; and the ranch was doing well. He'd be sorry to see it go, but luckily Thane would never know if Vivian were to leave the ranch and put it up for sale.

It was too bad that Mike couldn't afford to buy the ranch. When it went on the market, it would be out of his price range. The bad thing was if Clint Woodson were to buy it. If only there was a way to let certain people know and maybe do it when Clint was out of town. Mike shrugged. That would be up to Vivian. It wouldn't be his responsibility.

He should never have come to work on the ranch. He almost didn't, but he felt honor bound to keep his promise to Thane. Maybe that was why Thane had given him the money. He knew Mike could never have come home and gone to work at another ranch with the gift that Thane had given him.

If Thane only knew how everything had turned out, he wouldn't be so happy that he'd sent Mike to the Tumbling T Ranch.

Mike was glad he was going home soon to see his family. He was not looking forward to telling his mom about his baby, however. She wasn't going to be happy with him because she loved babies and this one would really not be with them a lot of the time. He dreaded telling her. He dreaded telling his brothers, too, but he knew they'd understand his feelings about Vivian and her future inheritance, her multimillionaire status now. They'd all been raised to take charge, take responsibility.

He decided right then and there to move out of the big house and back into the guesthouse. At least Sandy would come see him there. He had one month to go to keep his promise to Thane and then he was going to turn in his resignation and look elsewhere for a ranch job. Now, he had more experience as a foreman so that would be good.

He moved his things that evening out to the guesthouse, opening it up to let it air out after being closed up. There was no one living on the second floor in the main house now. At least some were still on the third floor. He was glad Thane couldn't know what was happening to his beloved ranch.

Mike changed clothes and went for a run, trying to keep busy, to wear himself down so he'd get a few hours of sleep. He jogged six miles and finally went back to move a few more of his things to the guesthouse. He went through the house until he found a small framed picture of Vivian. He wanted her picture in the guesthouse. He knew that wasn't the way to forget her or to get over her and maybe it was just because evening was setting in and he missed her more than ever. He carried the picture upstairs to get his own things.

As he gathered his boots and hats he had left behind, he glanced at his bed and remembered her there, smiling at him. Emotions racked him, pain and desire. He missed her so much and he wanted her. He wanted her laughter, her fun, her hot lovemaking, her gorgeous body. She was the mother of his baby. He was throwing all that away because of a bunch of money. Her money—no matter how much she had—was not more important than their love, being a family and raising and loving their baby. He needed to really think things through. Life changes. He had grown up with certain ideas about life, but maybe he needed to rethink and adapt before he lost what was the most important thing in his life— Vivian's love. Was he giving too much importance to her wealth? It hurt like hell to lose her. For the first time in his life, he wondered if he had fallen in love.

With each passing day, Vivian missed Mike more. She longed to see him, to feel his arms around her. She was going to have to sell the ranch, move to Dallas permanently. She would ask Thane's family if they wanted the ranch, but she didn't think any of them would, certainly not his father. She'd have to sell it. She thought of her studio there that she loved so much, the quiet days of painting. She had been happy there, but a baby would change everything and it wasn't going to work out for her to stay at the ranch.

She couldn't bear to think about selling the ranch because she knew Clint Woodson would immediately grab it up. She had to think about any way to avoid that happening. Even her neighbors had asked her not to let Clint buy it.

Thoughts of the ranch led to thoughts of her handsome foreman. She still mourned the loss of Thane and now she had added the pain of losing Mike. Would she have been better off if Thane hadn't hired him? She placed her hand on her flat stomach and thought about the precious baby she was going to have and knew her answer. She didn't have any regrets about Thane hiring Mike. His baby was growing inside her, and joy filled her every time she thought about it. A baby to love and cherish and watch grow up. Tears stung her eyes. If only Mike wanted this baby the way she did. If only he missed her the way she yearned for him.

He must miss her some, she realized, because he still called her even though she wasn't taking his calls.

She thought about what his old-fashioned narrow-mindedness was causing them both to give up, what he had to gain from his actions, what he must really feel. Why would he keep calling her if he wasn't interested in her? Maybe she ought to talk to Mike one more time. He had tried to call several times but she hadn't answered because she was avoiding the pain she had felt after talking to him. She knew it wasn't about business because if it was business, he would just call Henry and tell him to tell her.

Maybe she should go to the ranch and have a talk with Mike and see if he still felt the same about her money now that they had been apart awhile. She sat mulling over whether to go back to the ranch or not. Was she just fooling herself and trying to find an excuse to see Mike? She better decide because she suspected that soon he would be gone. Should she call him and tell him she wanted to come see him or just go?

While she thought about it, her phone rang.

She answered and heard Mike's voice. "I'm about a block away. Is it convenient to come see you now?"

Startled, she glanced in the mirror. "Yes, you can come see me. I'll call downstairs and give them your name so you can come up."

"I'll see you in a few minutes."

Curious and wondering about what he wanted, she raced into the bedroom to yank off her T-shirt and cutoffs. She pulled on a red cotton sleeveless blouse and matching red linen slacks and sandals. She ran a brush through her hair and was picking up the room when she heard the bell that indicated someone was coming up in the elevator. She went to the entryway and waited to see him.

It seemed to take forever before the elevator doors opened and he stood before her.

He looked so incredibly handsome in his black Stetson, black boots, his charcoal jacket, white shirt and crisp jeans. Her heart thudded and it was an effort to resist reaching out to hug and kiss him.

"This is a surprise," she said instead.

"I've tried to call you."

"I know. I should have taken your calls. Come in."

He carried a small white box in his hands and she wondered why he was in Dallas.

"I've been thinking about us," he said, stopping only a few feet into her condo and turning to face her. "You look gorgeous."

"You look rather good yourself. I might have looked a little bit better if you'd told me you were coming."

"You look wonderful. I brought you a present because I've missed you," he said, holding out the white box. It was tied with a white satin bow.

Her heart pounded and she stared at him in surprise. She took the box from his hands. "I've missed you, too, Mike," she said, gazing into his green eyes and wanting to toss aside the box and throw herself into his arms.

"I hope you like it," he said, glancing at the present in her hands that she had forgotten about—mainly because she was envisioning kissing him. He obviously wanted her to open it, so she untied the bow and opened the box to stare at a gold ring with a dazzling huge diamond surrounded by sparkling smaller ones. She looked up at him in question. "This is beautiful," she whispered. "But—"

He tossed his hat and jacket away and stepped close to take the ring and hold her hand. "Vivian Warner, I love you with all my heart and I want to marry you. Will you marry me?"

Tears filled her eyes. "You've never said you love me," she whispered while her heart pounded.

"I didn't know I did until you left and I hurt without you. I think about you, miss you and want you every minute. All the joy has gone out of my life and off the ranch." He took her other hand in his. "Vivian, I love you. Will you marry me?"

She watched him put the ring on her finger, unable to believe that this was happening, that he was here saying these things she'd longed to hear. "It's beautiful."

"You're beautiful and I need you. I love you with all my heart and I just didn't realize or recognize what I felt until you were gone."

She looked at the ring on her finger, but she was still holding her breath.

"Mike, what about the money?"

"Oh, hell, it's money. It's pieces of paper. I figured there must be some way to work this out. I can live on mine and you can live on yours or whatever you want to do. As you said, it's a pile of money, but it's not as important as love and people. You're the woman I love and you're carrying our baby whom we'll love, and we'll have more babies. So maybe I have been a little too hardheaded and obtuse and—"

She threw her arms around his neck and kissed him, her heart thumping wildly with joy. She leaned back laughing. "Oh, yes, my love, my handsome cowboy, I love you and I will marry you."

He gave a whoop and twirled her around. Then he kissed her, his lips never leaving hers until he'd carried her to her bedroom. He stood her on her feet and as if by magic their clothes disappeared. All she was aware of was Mike in her arms, his lips on hers and he loved her.

"Mike, I'm so happy. I love you with all my heart. You're wonderful. You're not an alpha male right now."

"Ha, that's what you think, darlin'. But I'm not

when it comes to pleasing my woman. I want to make you happy. I love you so much. I can't tell you how awful it's been without you at the ranch."

The reminder pulled her up. "The ranch. Mike, I was getting ready to sell it."

"And I was getting ready to quit. Well, we'll both have to change our plans and—" He stopped and shrugged. "Except I've already promised Lewis Owens the foreman job. Now what the hell am I going to do?"

She giggled. "Make love to the owner."

"Vivian," he said as she nuzzled his neck, trailing kisses to his ear. "Get serious."

She looked up at him. "I know exactly what you're going to do. Just a minute, Mike." She slipped out of his arms and disappeared into the closet. She came back with the torn, wrinkled brown paper that had been in the packet Thane had given Mike to give to her.

Mike raised his eyebrows. "What?"

"Look on the back of this paper that was wrapped around my diamond pendant. It's Thane's handwriting. Read it."

She handed the paper to Mike and he read aloud: "Vivian, I love you. Love Mike. He will take care of you and the ranch. T."

She placed her hand over his. "I know what we'll do. We'll marry. We'll have a small wedding, just our families and closest friends and the ranch people."

"Yeah, that's a small wedding—about three hundred."

She smiled. "That's okay. And after we marry, we'll put the ranch in both our names and you'll be the owner like Thane was. Lewis will be our foreman, the way Slade was, and he'll work for you just like he's doing now. And I'll be a mama for our baby and our babies. Plus I'll be an artist and your wife." She looked at him, knowing all her love shone in her eyes for him to see. "What do you think?"

He gazed at her solemnly and looked at the note in his hand. "I think Thane had a premonition he wouldn't make it home. He covered his bases. The money he gave me was enough that I'd be obliged to stay the three months. He knew that. By then he knew I'd be hooked. I think he wanted us to fall in love if he didn't make it home because I'd take care of you and take care of the ranch. And when you cry over Thane, I won't be jealous because I'll cry with you. I loved him, too. He was the best friend possible and I'm sure he was a good husband to you."

"Like you will be."

"For as long as I live." He pulled her to him, wrapping her in his strong arms. "I didn't do so well catching on that I was in love, but it's the first time I've ever been in love. And the last." He kissed her.

It wasn't the most passionate kiss Mike had ever given her, nor the longest, but it was the best because it came with a declaration of his love.

When he broke the kiss, he asked a favor. "One of our fellow rangers, Noah Grant, is getting out of the service next month. I'd like to wait to have the wedding so we can include him. He was important to Thane, and to me."

"Of course, we can include him."

"I'll have to meet your family and you'll have to meet mine—soon, if we want to have the wedding next month and get on with life."

"I think so," she said dreamily, holding her hand up to twist it and admire her ring. She looked at him. "I want to hear the 'I love you' part again."

He took her hand in his and gazed into her eyes. "My darlin' Vivian, I love you with all my heart. I love you now and forever."

"That is so wonderful," she said, smiling at him. "And I love you, Mike Moretti, with all my heart. Mike, I'm so happy. I've loved you for a long time."

"Well, you didn't tell me."

"I would think not, when I didn't hear any words of love from you."

"Well, darlin', all that's about to change. Now that I realize what love is, I'll be telling you every day of my life."

"Oh, I'm so glad. I love you, my old-fashioned alpha male who stopped being one long enough to win my heart and find love."

He shrugged. "I don't have an alpha male bone left in my body. Well, maybe one."

She giggled and hugged him. "You've made me so happy. If Thane couldn't come home, this is what he would have wanted."

"I think you're right, Vivian. He was looking out

for you, that ranch and maybe me. We have to name the first boy Thane."

"I agree," she said, holding Mike tightly while she kissed him and felt showered with love and blessings and fulfillment.

* * * * *

If you loved this Texas-set romance from
USA TODAY bestselling author Sara Orwig,
pick up these other titles!

The Texan's Contract Marriage
One Texas Night...
Her Texan to Tame
The Texan's Forbidden Fiancée
Expecting the Rancher's Child

Available now from Harlequin Desire!

If you're on Twitter, tell us what you think of
Harlequin Desire! #harlequindesire

*Can a former bad boy and the woman
he never forgot find true love during one
unforgettable Christmas?
Find out in CHRISTMASTIME COWBOY,
the sizzling new* COPPER RIDGE *novel from*
New York Times *bestselling author Maisey Yates.
Read on for your sneak peek...*

LIAM DONNELLY WAS nobody's favorite.

Though being a favorite in their household growing up would never have meant much, Liam was confident that as much as both of his parents disdained their younger son, Alex, they hated Liam more.

And as much as his brothers loved him—or whatever you wanted to call their brand of affection—Liam knew he wasn't the one they'd carry out if there was a house fire. That was fine, too.

It wasn't self-pity. It was just a fact.

But while he wasn't anyone's particular favorite, he knew he was at least one person's least favorite.

Sabrina Leighton hated him with every ounce of her beautiful, petite being. Not that he blamed her. But, considering they were having a business meeting today, he did hope that she could keep some of the hatred bottled up.

Liam got out of his truck and put his cowboy hat

on, surveying his surroundings. The winery spread was beautiful, with a large, picturesque house overlooking the grounds. The winery and the road leading up to it were carved in to an Oregon mountainside. Trees and forest surrounded the facility on three sides, creating a secluded feeling. Like the winery was part of another world. In front of the first renovated barn was a sprawling lawn and a path that led down to the river. There was a seating area there and Liam knew that during the warmer months it was a nice place to hang out. Right now, it was too damned cold, and the damp air that blew up from the rushing water sent a chill straight through him.

He shoved his hands in his pockets and kept on walking. There were three rustic barns on the property that they used for weddings and dinners, and one that had been fully remodeled in to a dining and tasting room.

He had seen the new additions online. He hadn't actually been to Grassroots Winery in the past thirteen years. That was part of the deal. The deal that had been struck back when Jamison Leighton was still owner of the place.

Back when Liam had been nothing more than a good-for-nothing, low-class troublemaker with a couple of misdemeanors to his credit.

Times changed.

Liam might still be all those things at heart, but he was also a successful businessman. And Jamison Leighton no longer owned Grassroots.

Some things, however, hadn't changed. The presence of Sabrina Leighton being one of them.

It had been thirteen years. But he couldn't pretend he thought everything was all right and forgiven. Not considering the way she had reacted when she had seen him at Ace's bar the past few months.

Small towns. Like everybody was at the same party and could only avoid each other for so long.

If it wasn't at the bar, they would most certainly end up at a four-way stop at the same time, or in the same aisle at the grocery store.

But today's meeting would not be accidental. Today's meeting was planned. He wondered if something would get thrown at him. It certainly wouldn't be the first time.

He walked across the gravel lot and into the dining room. It was empty, since the facility—a rustic barn with a wooden chandelier hanging in the center—had yet to open for the day. There was a bar with stools positioned at the front, and tables set up around the room. Back when he had worked here, there had been one basic tasting room, and nowhere for anyone to sit. Most of the wine had been sent out to retail stores for sale, rather than making the winery itself some kind of destination.

He wondered when all of that had changed. He imagined it had something to do with Lindy, the new owner and ex-wife of Jamison Leighton's son, Damien. As far as Liam knew, and he knew enough—considering he didn't get involved with business ventures without figuring out what he was getting into—Damien had drafted the world's dumbest prenuptial agreement. At least, it was dumb for a man who clearly had problems keeping his dick in his pants.

Though why Sabrina was still working at the winery when her sister-in-law had current ownership, and her brother had been deposed, and her parents were—from what he had read in public records—apoplectic about the loss of their family legacy, he didn't know. But he assumed he would find out. At about the same time he found out whether or not something was going to get thrown at his head.

The door from the back opened, and he gritted his teeth. Because, no matter how prepared he felt philosophically to see Sabrina, he knew that there would be impact. There always was. A damned funny thing, that one woman could live in the back of his mind the way she had for so long. That no matter how many years or how many women he put between them, she still burned bright and hot in his memory.

That no matter that he had steeled himself to run into her—because he knew how small towns worked—the impact was like a brick to the side of his head every single time.

She appeared a moment after the door opened, looking severe. Overly so. Her blond hair was pulled back into a high ponytail, and she was wearing a black sheath dress that went down past her knees but conformed to curves that were more generous than they'd been thirteen years ago.

In a good way.

"Hello, Liam," she said, her tone impersonal. Had she not used his first name, it might have been easy to pretend that she didn't know who he was.

"Sabrina."

"Lindy told me that you wanted to talk about a potential joint venture. And since that falls under my jurisdiction as manager of the tasting room, she thought we might want to work together."

Now she was smiling.

The smile was so brittle it looked like it might crack her face.

"Yes, I'm familiar with the details. Particularly since this venture was my idea." He let a small silence hang there for a beat before continuing. "I'm looking at an empty building on the end of Main Street. It would be more than just a tasting room. It would be a small café with some retail space."

"How would it differ from Lane Donnelly's store? She already offers specialty foods."

"Well, we would focus on Grassroots wine and Laughing Irish cheese. Also, I would happily purchase products from Lane's to give the menu a local focus. The café would be nothing big. Just a small lunch place with wine. Very limited selection. Very specialty. But I feel like in a tourist location, that's what you want."

"Great," she said, her smile remaining completely immobile.

He took that moment to examine her more closely. The changes in her face over the years. She was more beautiful now than she had been at seventeen. Her slightly round, soft face had refined in the ensuing years, her cheekbones now more prominent, the angle of her chin sharper.

Her eyebrows looked different, too. When she'd been a teenager, they'd been thinner, rounder. Now they were a bit stronger, more angular.

"Great," he returned. "I guess we can go down and have a look at the space sometime this week. Gage West is the owner of the property, and he hasn't listed it yet. Handily, my sister-in-law is good friends with his wife. Both of my sisters-in-law, actually. So I got the inside track on that."

Her expression turned bland. "How impressive."

She sounded absolutely unimpressed. "It wasn't intended to be impressive. Just useful."

She sighed slowly. "Did you have a day of the week in mind to go view the property? Because I really am very busy."

"Are you?"

"Yes," she responded, that smile spreading over her face again. "This is a very demanding job, plus I do have a life."

She stopped short of saying exactly what that life entailed.

"Too busy to do this, which is part of your actual job?" he asked.

On the surface she looked calm, but he could sense a dark energy beneath that spoke of a need to savage him. "I had my schedule sorted out for the next couple of weeks. This is coming together more quickly than expected."

"I'll work something out with Gage and give Lindy a call, how about that?"

"You don't have to call Lindy. I'll give you my phone number. You can call or text me directly."

She reached over to the counter and took a card from the rustic surface, extending her hand toward him. He reached out and took the card, their finger-tips brushing as they made the handoff.

And he felt it. Straight down to his groin, where he had always felt things for her, even though it was impossible. Even though he was all wrong for her. And even though now they were doing a business deal together, and she looked like she would cheer-fully chew through his flesh if given half the chance.

She might be smiling, but he didn't trust that smile. He was still waiting. Waiting for her to shout recriminations at him now that they were alone. Every other time he had encountered her over the past four months it had been in public. Twice in Ace's bar, and once walking down the street, where she had made a very quick sharp left to avoid walking past him.

It had not been subtle, and it had certainly not spoken of somebody who was over the past.

So his assumption had been that if the two of them were ever alone she was going to let him have it. But she didn't. Instead, she gave him that card and then began to look…bored.

"Did you need anything else?" she asked.

"Not really. Though I have some spreadsheet information that you might want to look over. Ideas that I have for the layout, the menu. It is getting a little ahead of ourselves, in case we end up not liking the venue."

"You've been to look at the venue already, haven't you?" It was vaguely accusatory.

"I have been there, yes. But again, I believe in preparedness. I was hardly going to get very deep into this if I didn't think it was viable. Personally, I'm interested in making sure that we have diverse interests. The economy doesn't typically favor farms, Sabrina. And that is essentially what my brothers and I have. I expect an uphill fight to make that place successful."

She tilted her head to the side. "Like you said, you do your research."

Her friendliness was beginning to slip. And he waited. For something else. For something to get thrown at him. It didn't happen.

"That I do. Take these," he said, handing her the folder that he was holding on to. He made sure their fingers didn't touch this time. "And we'll talk next week."

Then he turned and walked away from her, and he resisted the strong impulse to turn back and get one more glance at her. It wasn't the first time he had resisted that.

He had a feeling it wouldn't be the last.

As SOON AS Liam walked out of the tasting room, Sabrina let out a breath that had been killing her to keep in. A breath that contained about a thousand insults and recriminations. And more than a few very colorful swear word combinations. A breath that nearly burned her throat, because it was full of so many sharp and terrible things.

She lifted her hands to her face and realized they were shaking. It had been thirteen years. Why did he still affect her like this? Maybe, just maybe, if she had ever found a man who made her feel even half of what Liam did, she wouldn't have such a hard time dealing with him. The feelings wouldn't be so strong.

But she hadn't. So that supposition was basically moot.

The worst part was the tattoos. He'd had about three when he'd been nineteen. Now they covered both of his arms, and she had the strongest urge to make them as familiar to her as the original tattoos had been. To memorize each and every detail about them.

The tree was the one that really caught her attention. The Celtic knots, she knew, were likely a nod to his Irish heritage, but the tree—whose branches she could see stretching down from his shoulder—she was curious about what that meant.

"And you are spending too much time thinking about him," she admonished herself.

She shouldn't be thinking about him at all. She should just focus on congratulating herself for saying nothing stupid. At least she hadn't cried and demanded answers for the night he had completely laid waste to her every feeling.

"How did it go?"

Sabrina turned and saw her sister-in-law, Lindy, come in. People would be forgiven for thinking that she and Lindy were actually biological sisters. In fact, they looked much more alike than Sabrina and her younger sister Beatrix did.

Like Sabrina, Lindy had long, straight blond hair. Bea, on the other hand, had freckles all over her face and a wild riot of reddish-brown curls that resisted taming almost as strongly as the youngest Leighton sibling herself did.

That was another thing Sabrina and Lindy had in common. They were predominantly tame. At least, they kept things as together as they possibly could on the surface.

"Fine."

"You didn't savage him with a cheese knife?"

"Lindy," Sabrina said, "please. This is dry-clean

only." She waved her hand up and down, indicating her dress.

"I don't know what your whole issue is with him…"

Because no one spoke of it. Lindy had married Sabrina's brother after the unpleasantness. It was no secret that Sabrina and her father were estranged—even if it was a brittle, quiet estrangement. But unless Damien had told Lindy the details—and Sabrina doubted he knew all of them—her sister-in-law wouldn't know the whole story.

"I don't have an issue with him," Sabrina said. "I knew him thirteen years ago. That has nothing to do with now. It has nothing to do with this new venture for the winery. Which I am on board with one hundred percent." It was true. She was.

"Well," Lindy said, "that's good to hear."

She could tell that Lindy didn't believe her. "It's going to be fine. I'm looking forward to this." That was also true. Mostly. She was looking forward to expanding Grassroots. Looking forward to helping build the winery, and making it into something that was truly theirs. So that her parents could no longer shout recriminations about Lindy stealing something from the Leighton family.

Eventually, they would make the winery so much more successful that most of it would be theirs.

And if her own issues with her parents were tangled up in all of this, then…that was just how it was.

Sabrina wanted it all to work, and work well. If for

no other reason than to prove to Liam Donnelly that she was no longer the seventeen-year-old girl whose world he'd wrecked all those years ago.

In some ways, Sabrina envied the tangible ways in which Lindy had been able to exact revenge on Damien. Of course, Sabrina's relationship with Liam wasn't anything like a ten-year marriage ended by infidelity. She gritted her teeth. She did her best not to think about Liam. About the past. Because it hurt. Every damn time it hurt. It didn't matter if it should or not.

But now that he was back in Copper Ridge, now that she sometimes just happened to run into him, it was worse. It was harder not to think about him.

Him and the grand disaster that had happened after.

* * * * *

Look for CHRISTMASTIME COWBOY,
available from Maisey Yates and HQN Books
wherever books are sold.

COMING NEXT MONTH FROM

H HARLEQUIN®

Desire

Available December 5, 2017

#2557 HIS SECRET SON
The Westmoreland Legacy • by Brenda Jackson
The SEAL who fathered Bristol's son died a hero's death...or so she was told. But now Coop is back and vowing to claim his child! Her son deserves to know his father, so Bristol must find a way to fight temptation...and keep her heart safe.

#2558 BEST MAN UNDER THE MISTLETOE
Texas Cattleman's Club: Blackmail • by Jules Bennett
Planning a wedding with the gorgeous, sexy best man would have been a lot easier if he weren't Chelsea Hunt's second-worst enemy. Gabe Walsh is furious that the sins of his uncle have also fallen on him, but soon his desire to prove his innocence turns into the desire to make her his!

#2559 THE CHRISTMAS BABY BONUS
Billionaires and Babies • by Yvonne Lindsay
Getting snowed in with his sexy assistant is difficult enough. But when an abandoned baby is found in the stables, die-hard bachelor Piers may find himself yearning for a family for Christmas...

#2560 LITTLE SECRETS: HIS PREGNANT SECRETARY
Little Secrets • by Joanne Rock
After a heated argument with his secretary turns sexually explosive, entrepreneur Jager McNeill knows the right thing to do is propose... because now she's carrying his child! But what will he do when she won't settle for a marriage of convenience?

#2561 SNOWED IN WITH A BILLIONAIRE
Secrets of the A-List • by Karen Booth
Joy McKinley just *had* to be rescued by one of the wealthiest, sexiest men she's ever met. Especially when she's hiding out in someone else's house under a name that isn't hers. But when they get snowed in together, can their romance survive the truth?

#2562 BABY IN THE MAKING
Accidental Heirs • by Elizabeth Bevarly
Surprise heir Hannah Robinson will lose her fortune if she doesn't get pregnant. Enter daredevil entrepreneur Yeager Novak...and the child they'll make together! Opposites attract on this baby-making adventure, but will that be enough to turn their pact into a real romance?

HDCNM1117

Get 2 Free Books,
Plus 2 Free Gifts—
just for trying the Reader Service!

*Bane Westmoreland's SEAL team is made up of
sexy alpha males.*

Don't miss Laramie "Coop" Cooper's story
HIS SECRET SON
from New York Times bestselling author Brenda Jackson!

*The SEAL who fathered Bristol's son died a hero's death...or
so she was told. But now Coop is back and vowing to claim
his child! Her son deserves to know his father, so Bristol must
find a way to fight temptation...and keep her heart safe.*

Read on for a sneak peek at
HIS SECRET SON,
part of **THE WESTMORELAND LEGACY** *series.*

Laramie stared at Bristol. "You were pregnant?"

"Yes," she said in a soft voice. "And you're free to order a
paternity test if you need to verify that my son is yours."

He had a son? It took less than a second for his emotions to
go from shock to disbelief. "How?"

She lifted a brow. "Probably from making love almost
nonstop for three solid days."

They had definitely done that. Although he'd used a condom
each and every time, he knew there was always a possibility
that something could go wrong.

"And where is he?" he asked.

"At home."

Where the hell was that? It bothered him how little he knew about the woman who'd just announced she'd given birth to his child. At least she'd tried contacting him to let him know. Some women would not have done so.

If his child had been born nine months after their holiday fling, that meant he would have turned two in September. While Laramie was in a cell, somewhere in the world, Bristol had been giving life.

To his child.

Emotions Laramie had never felt before suddenly bombarded him with the impact of a Tomahawk missile. He was a parent, which meant he had to think about someone other than himself. He wasn't sure how he felt about that. But then, wasn't he used to taking care of others as a member of his SEAL team?

She nodded. "I'm not asking you for anything Laramie, if that's what you're thinking. I just felt you had a right to know about the baby."

She wasn't asking him for anything? Did she not know her bold declaration that he'd fathered her child demanded everything?

"I want to see him."

"You will. I would never keep Laramie from you."

"You named him Laramie?" Even more emotions swamped him. Her son—their son—had his name?

She hesitated. "Yes."

Then he asked, "So, what's your reason for giving yourself my last name, as well?"

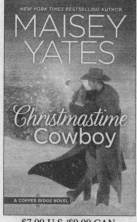

$7.99 U.S./$9.99 CAN.

EXCLUSIVE
Limited Time Offer

$1.⁰⁰ OFF

New York Times Bestselling Author
MAISEY YATES
Christmastime Cowboy

*It's Christmas in Copper Ridge,
and love is waiting to be unwrapped…*

*Available October 24, 2017.
Pick up your copy today!*

HQN™

$1.⁰⁰ OFF
**the purchase price of CHRISTMASTIME
COWBOY by Maisey Yates.**

Offer valid from October 24, 2017, to November 30, 2017.
Redeemable at participating retail outlets. Not redeemable at Barnes & Noble.
Limit one coupon per purchase. Valid in the U.S.A. and Canada only.

52615043

Canadian Retailers: Harlequin Enterprises Limited will pay the face value of this coupon plus 10.25¢ if submitted by customer for this product only. Any other use constitutes fraud. Coupon is nonassignable. Void if taxed, prohibited or restricted by law. Consumer must pay any government taxes. Void if copied. Inmar Promotional Services ("IPS") customers submit coupons and proof of sales to Harlequin Enterprises Limited, P.O. Box 31000, Scarborough, ON M1R 0E7, Canada. Non-IPS retailer—for reimbursement submit coupons and proof of sales directly to Harlequin Enterprises Limited, Retail Marketing Department, 225 Duncan Mill Rd., Don Mills, ON M3B 3K9, Canada.

5 65373 00076 2   (8100)0 12301

U.S. Retailers: Harlequin Enterprises Limited will pay the face value of this coupon plus 8¢ if submitted by customer for this product only. Any other use constitutes fraud. Coupon is nonassignable. Void if taxed, prohibited or restricted by law. Consumer must pay any government taxes. Void if copied. For reimbursement submit coupons and proof of sales directly to Harlequin Enterprises, Ltd 482, NCH Marketing Services, P.O. Box 880001, El Paso, TX 88588-0001, U.S.A. Cash value 1/100 cents.

® and ™ are trademarks owned and used by the trademark owner and/or its licensee.

© 2017 Harlequin Enterprises Limited

PHCOUPMYHD1117

LOVE
Harlequin
romance?

Join our Harlequin community to share your thoughts and connect with other romance readers!

Be the first to find out about promotions, news, and exclusive content!

Sign up for the Harlequin e-newsletter and download a free book from any series at

www.TryHarlequin.com

Want to give in to temptation with
steamy tales of irresistible desire?

Check out **Harlequin® Presents®**,
Harlequin® Desire and
Harlequin® Kimani™ Romance books!

New books available every month!

CONNECT WITH US AT:

Harlequin.com/Community

 Facebook.com/HarlequinBooks

 Twitter.com/HarlequinBooks

 Instagram.com/HarlequinBooks

 Pinterest.com/HarlequinBooks

ReaderService.com

**ROMANCE WHEN
YOU NEED IT**

PGENRE2017

HARLEQUIN®

A *Romance* FOR EVERY MOOD™

Love the Harlequin book you just read?

Your opinion matters.

Review this book on your favorite book site, review site, blog or your own social media properties and share your opinion with other readers!